hC

'**But you do want me, Liana,**' Sandro said softly. '**You want me very much. And even if you try to deny it I'll know. I'll feel your response in your lips that open to mine, in your hands that reach for me, in your body that responds to me.**'

'I know that,' she choked. 'I'm not denying anything.'

She turned her face with all its naked emotion away from him.

'No,' he agreed, his voice as hard as iron now, as hard as his gunmetal-grey eyes. 'You're not denying it. You're just resisting it with every fibre of your being. Resisting me.'

She let out a shudder and he shook his head.

'Why, Liana? You agreed to this marriage, as I did. Why can't we find this pleasurable at least?'

'Because…'

Because she wasn't strong enough. She'd open herself up to him just a little and a tidal wave of emotion would rush through her. She wouldn't be able to hold it back and it would devastate her. She knew it instinctively—knew that giving in just a little to Sandro would crack her right open, shatter her into pieces. She'd never come together again.

How could she explain all of that?

THE DIOMEDI HEIRS

Who will become the next King of Maldinia?

The world's media is waiting with bated breath
for the estranged Diomedi Princes to be reunited
and the rightful King—with his chosen Queen—
to be seated upon the throne!

Read Prince Leo's story in:
THE PRINCE SHE NEVER KNEW

To restore the reputation of the monarchy,
darkly brooding **Prince Leo** has sacrificed everything.
His marriage might be for show, but the feelings
his new bride Alyse evokes in him are threatening
his iron-clad control.

Read Prince Alessandro's story in:
A QUEEN FOR THE TAKING?

Black sheep **Prince Alessandro** has returned home
to claim the throne—and the woman he discarded
years ago—but he meets his match in
the woman Liana has now become!

A QUEEN FOR THE TAKING?

BY
KATE HEWITT

Published in Great Britain 2014
by Mills & Boon, an imprint of Harlequin (UK) Limited,
Eton House, 18-24 Paradise Road, Richmond, Surrey, TW9 1SR

© 2014 Kate Hewitt

ISBN: 978 0 263 24179 2

Harlequin (UK) Limited's policy is to use papers that are natural, renewable and recyclable products and made from wood grown in sustainable forests. The logging and manufacturing processes conform to the legal environmental regulations of the country of origin.

Printed and bound in Great Britain
by CPI Antony Rowe, Chippenham, Wiltshire

Kate Hewitt discovered her first Mills & Boon® romance on a trip to England when she was thirteen, and she's continued to read them ever since. She wrote her first story at the age of five, simply because her older brother had written one and she thought she could do it too. That story was one sentence long— fortunately they've become a bit more detailed as she's grown older. She has written plays, short stories and magazine serials for many years, but writing romance remains her first love. Besides writing, she enjoys reading, travelling and learning to knit.

After marrying the man of her dreams—her older brother's childhood friend—she lived in England for six years, and now resides in Connecticut with her husband, her three young children and the possibility of one day getting a dog.

Kate loves to hear from readers—you can contact her through her website: www.kate-hewitt.com

Recent titles by the same author:

THE PRINCE SHE NEVER KNEW
  (The Diomedi Heirs)
HIS BRAND OF PASSION
  (The Bryants: Powerful & Proud)
IN THE HEAT OF THE SPOTLIGHT
  (The Bryants: Powerful & Proud)
BENEATH THE VEIL OF PARADISE
  (The Bryants: Powerful & Proud)

**Did you know these are also available as eBooks?
Visit www.millsandboon.co.uk**

CHAPTER ONE

ALESSANDRO DIOMEDI, KING of Maldinia, opened the door to the opulent reception room and gazed resolutely upon the woman intended to be his bride. Liana Aterno, the daughter of the duke of Abruzzo, stood in the centre of the room, her body elegant and straight, her gaze clear and steady and even cold. She looked remarkably composed, considering the situation.

Carefully Sandro closed the door, the final click seeming to sound the end of his freedom. But no, that was being fanciful, for his freedom had surely ended six months ago, when he'd left his life in California to return to Maldinia and accept his place as first in line to the throne. Any tattered remnant of it had gone when he'd buried his father and taken his place as king.

'Good afternoon.' His voice seemed to echo through the large room with its gilt walls and frescoed ceilings, the only furniture a few ornate tables of gold and marble set against the walls. Not exactly the most welcoming of spaces, and for a moment Sandro wished he'd specified to put Lady Liana into a more comfortable chamber.

Although, he acknowledged cynically, considering the nature of their imminent discussion—and probable relationship—perhaps this room was appropriate.

'Good afternoon, Your Highness.' She didn't curtsey,

which he was glad of, because he hated all the osten-
tatious trappings of royalty and obeisance, but she did
bend her head in a gesture of respect so for a moment he
could see the bare, vulnerable nape of her neck. It almost
made him soften. Then she lifted her head and pinned
him with that cold, clear-eyed gaze and he felt his heart
harden once more. He didn't want this. He never would.
But she obviously did.

'You had a pleasant journey?'

'Yes, thank you.'

He took a step into the room, studying her. He supposed she was pretty, if you liked women who were colourless. Her hair was so blonde it appeared almost white,
and she wore it pulled back in a tight chignon, a few
wispy tendrils coming to curl about her small, pearl-
studded ears.

She was slight, petite, and yet she carried herself with
both pride and grace, and wore a modest, high-necked,
long-sleeved dress of pale blue silk belted tightly at the
waist, an understated strand of pearls at her throat. She
had folded her hands at her waist like some pious nun
and stood calmly under his obvious scrutiny, accepting
his inspection with a cool and even haughty confidence.
All of it made him angry.

'You know why you're here.'

'Yes, Your Highness.'

'You can dispense with the titles. Since we are considering marriage, you may call me Alessandro, or Sandro,
whichever you prefer.'

'And which do you prefer?'

'You may call me Sandro.' Her composed compliance
annoyed him, although he knew such a reaction was un-
reasonable, even unjust. Yet he still felt it, felt the deep-
seated desire to wipe that cool little smile off her face

and replace it with something real. To feel something real himself.

But he'd left real emotions—honesty, understanding, all of it—behind in California. There was no place for them here, even when discussing his marriage.

'Very well,' she answered evenly, yet she didn't call him anything; she simply waited. Annoyance warred with reluctant amusement and even admiration. Did she have more personality than he'd initially assumed, or was she simply that assured of their possible nuptials?

Their marriage was virtually a sealed deal. He'd invited her to Maldinia to begin negotiations, and she'd agreed with an alacrity he'd found far too telling. So the duke's daughter wanted to be a queen. What a surprise. Another woman on a cold-hearted quest for money, power, and fame.

Love, of course, wouldn't enter into it. It never did; he'd learned that lesson too many times already.

Sandro strode farther into the room, his hands shoved into the pockets of his suit trousers. He walked to the window that looked out on the palace's front courtyard, the gold-tipped spikes of the twelve-foot-high fence that surrounded the entire grounds making his throat tighten. *Such a prison.* And one he'd reentered willingly. One he'd returned to with a faint, frail hope in his heart that had blown to so much cold ash when he'd actually seen his father again, after fifteen years.

I had no choice. If I could have, I'd have left you to rot in California, or, better yet, in hell.

Sandro swallowed and turned away.

'Tell me why you're here, Lady Liana.' He wanted to hear it from her own mouth, those tightly pursed lips.

A slight pause, and then she answered, her voice low

and steady. 'To discuss the possibility of a marriage between us.'

'Such a possibility does not distress or concern you,
considering we have never even met before?'

Another pause, even slighter, but Sandro still felt it.
'We have met before, Your Highness. When I was twelve.'

'Twelve.' He turned around to inspect her once again,
but her cold blonde beauty didn't trigger any memories.
Had she possessed such icy composure, as well as a resolute determination to be queen, at twelve years old? It
seemed likely. 'You are to call me Sandro, remember.'

'Of course.'

He almost smiled at that. Was she provoking him on
purpose? He'd rather that than the icy, emotionless composure. Any emotion was better than none.

'Where did we meet?'

'At a birthday party for my father in Milan.'

He didn't remember the event, but that didn't really
surprise him. If she'd been twelve, he would have been
twenty, and about to walk away from his inheritance,
his very self, only to return six months ago, when duty
demanded he reclaim his soul—or sell it. He still wasn't
sure which he'd done. 'And you remembered me?'

For a second, no more, she looked…not disconcerted,
but something close to it. Something distressing. Shadows flickered in her eyes, which, now that he'd taken a
step closer to her, he saw were a rather startling shade
of lavender. She wasn't so colourless, after all. Then she
blinked it back and nodded. 'Yes, I did.'

'I'm sorry to say I don't remember you.'

She shrugged, her shoulders barely twitching. 'I
wouldn't have expected you to. I was little more than
a child.'

He nodded, his gaze still sweeping over her, wondering what thoughts and feelings lurked behind that careful, blank mask of a face. What emotion had shadowed her eyes for just a moment?

Or was he being fanciful, sentimental? He had been before. He'd thought he'd learned the lessons, but perhaps he hadn't.

Liana Aterno had been one of the first names to come up in diplomatic discussions after his father had died, and he'd accepted that he must marry and provide an heir—and soon.

She was related to royalty, had devoted her life to charity work, and her father was prominent in finance and had held various important positions in the European Union—all of which Sandro had to consider, for the sake of his country. She was eminently and irritatingly suitable in every way. The perfect queen consort—and she looked as if she knew it.

'You have not considered other alliances in the meantime?' he asked. 'Other…relationships?' He watched her pale, heart-shaped face, no emotion visible in her eyes, no tightening of her mouth, no tension apparent in her lithe body. The woman reminded him of a statue, something made of cold, lifeless marble.

No, he realised, what she really reminded him of was his mother. An icy, beautiful bitch: emotionless, soulless, caring only about wealth and status and fame. About being queen.

Was that who this woman really was? Or was he being stupidly judgmental and entirely unfair, based on his own sorry experience? It was impossible to tell what she felt from her carefully blank expression, yet he felt a gut-deep revulsion to the fact that she was here at all, that she'd accepted his summons and was prepared to marry a stranger.

Just as he was.

'No,' she said after a moment. 'I have not…' She gave a slight shrug of her shoulders. 'I have devoted myself to charity work.'

Queen or nun. It was a choice women in her elevated position had had to make centuries before, but it seemed archaic now. Absurd.

And yet it was her reality, and very close to his. King or CEO of his own company. Slave or free.

'No one else?' he pressed. 'I have to admit, I am surprised. You're— What? Twenty-eight years old?' She gave a slight nod. 'Surely you've had other offers. Other relationships.'

Her mouth tightened, eyes narrowing slightly. 'As I said, I have devoted myself to charity work.'

'You can devote yourself to charity work and still be in a relationship,' he pointed out. 'Still marry.'

'Indeed, I hope so, Your Highness.'

A noble sentiment, he supposed, but one he didn't trust. Clearly only queen would do for this icy, ambitious woman.

Sandro shook his head slowly. Once he'd dreamed of a marriage, a relationship built on love, filled with passion and humour and joy. Once.

Gazing at her now, he knew she would make an able queen, a wonderful queen—clearly she'd been grooming herself for such a role. And the decision of his marriage was not about desire or choice. It was about duty, a duty he'd wilfully and shamefully ignored for far too long already.

He gave a brisk nod. 'I have obligations in the palace for the rest of this afternoon, but I would like us to have dinner together tonight, if you are amenable.'

She nodded, accepting, unsmiling. 'Of course, Your Highness.'

'We can get to know each other a bit better, perhaps, as well as discuss the practical aspects of this union.'

Another nod, just as swift and emotionless. 'Of course.'

He stared at her hard, wanting her to show some kind of emotion, whether it was uncertainty or hope or simple human interest. He saw nothing in her clear violet gaze, nothing but cool purpose, hard-hearted determination. Suppressing a stab of disappointment, he turned from the room. 'I'll send one of my staff in to see to your needs. Enjoy your stay in the palace of Averne, Lady Liana.'

'Thank you, Your Highness.'

It wasn't until he'd closed the door behind him that he realised she'd never called him Sandro.

Liana let out a long, slow breath and pressed her hands to her middle, relieved that the fluttering had stopped. She felt reassuringly calm now, comfortingly numb. So she'd met Alessandro Diomedi, king of Maldinia. Her future husband.

She crossed to the window and gazed out at the palace courtyard and the ancient buildings of Averne beyond the ornate fence, all framed by a cloudless blue sky. The snow-capped peaks of the Alps were just visible if she craned her neck.

She let out another breath and willed the tension to dissipate from her body. That whole conversation with King Alessandro had been surreal; she'd almost felt as if she'd been floating somewhere up by the ceiling, looking down at these two people, strangers who had never met before, at least not properly. And now they intended to marry each other.

She shook her head slowly, the realisation of what her future would hold still possessing the power to surprise and even unnerve her although it had been several weeks since her parents had suggested she consider Alessandro's suit.

He's a king, Liana, and you should marry. Have children of your own.

She'd never thought to marry, have children. The responsibility and risk were both too great. But she knew it was what her parents wanted, and a convenient marriage, at least, meant a loveless one. A riskless one.

So marry she would, if King Alessandro would have her. She took a deep breath as the flutters started again, reminded herself of the advantages of such a union.

As queen she could continue to devote herself to her charity work, and raise the profile of Hands To Help. Her position would benefit it so much, and she could not turn away from that, just as she could not turn away from her parents' wishes for her life.

She owed them too much.

Really, she told herself, it was perfect. It would give her everything she wanted—everything she would let herself want.

Except it didn't seem the king wanted it. *Her.* She recalled the slightly sneering, incredulous tone, the way he'd looked at her with a kind of weary derision. She didn't please him. Or was it simply marriage that didn't please him?

With a wary unease she recalled his sense of raw, restless power, as if this palace could not contain him, as if his emotions and ideas would bubble over, spill forth.

She wasn't used to that. Her parents were quiet, reserved people, and she had learned to be even more quiet and reserved than they were. To be invisible.

The only time she let herself be heard was when she was giving a public address for Hands To Help. On stage, talking about what the charity did, she had the words to say and the confidence to say them.

But with King Alessandro? With him looking at her as if… Almost as if he didn't even *like* her?

Words had deserted her. She'd cloaked herself in the cool, numbing calm she'd developed over the years, her only way of staying sane. Of surviving, because giving into emotion meant giving into the grief and guilt, and if she did that she knew she'd be lost. She'd drown in the feelings she'd never let herself acknowledge, much less express.

And King Alessandro, of all people, wasn't meant to call them up. This marriage was meant to be *convenient.* Cold. She wouldn't have agreed to it otherwise.

And yet the questions he'd asked her hadn't been either. And the doubt his voicing of them stirred up in her made her insides lurch with panic.

Tell me why you're here, Lady Liana…. Such a possibility does not distress or concern you, considering we have never even met before?

He'd almost sounded as if he *wanted* her to be distressed by the prospect of their marriage.

Perhaps she should have told him that she was.

Except, of course, she wasn't. Wouldn't be. Marriage to King Alessandro made sense. Her parents wanted it. She wanted the visibility for Hands To Help. It was the right choice. It had to be.

And yet just the memory of the king's imposing figure, all restless, rangy muscle and sinewy grace, made her insides quiver and jump. He wore his hair a little too long, ink-black and streaked with silver at the temples, carelessly rumpled as if he'd driven his fingers through it.

His eyes were iron-grey, hard and yet compelling. She'd had to work not to quell under that steely gaze, especially when his mouth had twisted with what had looked—and felt—like derision.

What about her displeased him?

What did he want from her, if not a practical and accepting approach to this marriage?

Liana didn't want to answer that question. She didn't even want to ask it. She had hoped they would be in agreement about this marriage, or as much as they could considering she hadn't wanted to marry at all.

But then perhaps King Alessandro didn't either. Perhaps his seeming resentment was at the situation, rather than his intended bride. Liana's lips formed a grim smile. Two people who had no desire to be married and yet would soon be saying their vows. Well, hopefully they wouldn't actually be seeing all that much of each other.

'Lady Liana?'

She turned to see one of the palace's liveried staff, his face carefully neutral, standing in the doorway. 'Yes?'

'The king requested that I show you to your room, so you may refresh yourself.'

'Thank you.' With a brisk nod she followed the man out of the ornate receiving room and down a long, marble-floored corridor to the east wing of the palace. He took her up a curving marble staircase with an impressive gold bannister, and then down yet another marble corridor until he finally arrived at a suite of rooms.

During the entire journey she'd only seen more staff, liveried and stony faced, giving her the uneasy sense that she was alone in this vast building save for the countless nameless employees. She wondered where the king had gone, or, for that matter, the queen dowager. Surely Sandro's mother, Sophia, intended to receive her?

Although, Liana acknowledged, she couldn't assume anything. The summons to Maldinia's royal palace had come so quickly and suddenly, a letter with Alessandro's royal insignia on top, its few pithy sentences comprising the request for Lady Liana Aterno of Abruzzo to discuss the possibility of marriage. Liana had been in shock; her mother, full of expectation.

This would be so good for you, Liana. You should marry. Why not Alessandro? Why not a king?

Why not, indeed? Her parents were traditional, even old-fashioned. Daughters married, produced heirs. It was perhaps an archaic idea in this modern world, but they clung to it.

And she couldn't let them down in their hopes for her. She owed them that much at least. She owed them so much more.

'These will be your rooms for your stay here, my lady. If you need anything, simply press the bell by the door and someone will come to your attention.'

'Thank you,' Liana murmured, and stepped into the sumptuous set of rooms. After ensuring she had no further requirements, the staff member left with a quiet click of the door. Liana gazed around the huge bedroom, its opulence a far cry from her modest apartment in Milan.

Acres of plush carpet stretched in every direction, and in the centre of the room, on its own dais, stood a magnificent canopied four-poster bed, piled high with silk pillows. The bed faced a huge stone fireplace with elaborate scrollwork, and several deep armchairs in blue patterned silk flanked it. It was a chilly March day and a fire had already been laid and lit, and now crackled cheerfully in the huge hearth.

Slowly Liana walked towards the fireplace and stretched her hands out to the flames. Her hands were icy; they always went cold when she was nervous. And despite her every attempt to convey the opposite to King Alessandro, she *had* been nervous.

She hadn't expected to be, had assumed a marriage such as theirs would be conducted like a corporate merger, their introduction no more than a business meeting. She wasn't naive; she knew what marriage would entail. Alessandro needed an heir.

But she hadn't expected his energy, his emotion. He'd been the opposite of her in every way: restless, quick-tempered, seething with something she didn't understand.

She closed her eyes, wished briefly that she could return to the simple life she'd made for herself working at the foundation, living in Milan, going out on occasion with friends. It probably didn't look like much to most people, but she'd found a soothing enjoyment in those small things. That was all she'd ever wanted, all she'd ever asked for. The safety of routines had calmed and comforted her, and just one meeting with Sandro Diomedi had ruffled up everything inside her.

Swallowing hard, she opened her eyes. *Enough.* Her life was not her own, and hadn't been since she was eight years old. She accepted that as the price she must pay, *should* pay.

But she wouldn't think anymore about that. It was as if there were a door in Liana's mind, and it clanged shut by sheer force of will. She wouldn't think about Chiara.

She turned away from the fire, crossing to the window to gaze out at the bare gardens still caught in the chill of late winter. Strange to think this view would become familiar when she was wed. This palace, this life, would all become part of her normal existence.

As would the king. *Sandro.*

She suppressed a shiver. What would marriage to King

Alessandro look like? She had a feeling it wouldn't look or feel like she'd assumed. Convenient. Safe.

She'd never even had a proper boyfriend, never been kissed except for a few quick, sloppy attempts on a couple dates she'd gone on over the years, pressured by her parents to meet a boy, fall in love, even though she hadn't been interested in either.

But Alessandro would want more than a kiss, and with him she felt it would be neither sloppy nor quick.

She let out a soft huff of laughter, shaking her head at herself. How on earth would she know how Alessandro would kiss?

But you'll find out soon enough.

She swallowed hard, the thought alone enough to make her palms go icy again. She didn't want to think about that, not yet.

She gazed around the bedroom, the afternoon stretching emptily in front of her. She couldn't bear to simply sit and wait in her room; she preferred being busy and active. She'd take a walk through the palace gardens, she decided. The fresh air would be welcome.

She dressed casually but carefully in wool trousers of pale grey and a twin set in mauve cashmere, the kind of bland, conservative clothes she'd chosen for ever.

She styled her hair, leaving it down, and did her discreet make-up and jewellery—pearls, as she always wore. It took her nearly an hour before she was ready, and then as soon as she left her room one of the staff standing to attention in the endless corridor hurried towards her.

'My lady?'

'I'd like to go outside, please. To have a stroll around the gardens if I may.'

'Very good, my lady.'

She followed the man in his blue-and-gold-tasselled

uniform down the corridor and then down several others and finally to a pair of French windows that led to a wide terrace with shallow steps leading to the gardens.

'Would you like an escort—?' he began, but Liana shook her head.

'No, thank you. I'll just walk around by myself.'

She breathed in the fresh, pine-scented mountain air as she took the first twisting path through the carefully clipped box hedges. Even though the palace was in the centre of Maldinia's capital city of Averne, it was very quiet in the gardens, the only sound the rustle of the wind through the still-bare branches of the trees and shrubs.

Liana dug her hands into the pockets of her coat, the chilly wind stinging her cheeks, glad for an afternoon's respite from the tension of meeting with the king. As she walked she examined the flowerbeds, trying to identify certain species although it was difficult with everything barely in blossom.

The sun was starting to sink behind the snow-capped peaks on the horizon when Liana finally turned back to the palace. She needed to get ready for her dinner with the king, and already she felt her brief enjoyment of the gardens replaced by a wary concern over the coming evening.

She could not afford to make a single misstep, and yet as she walked back towards the French windows glinting in the late afternoon sun she realised how little information King Alessandro had given her. Was this dinner a formal occasion with members of state, or something smaller and more casual? Would the queen be dining with them, or other members of the royal family? Liana knew that Alessandro's brother, Leo, and his wife, Alyse, lived in Averne, as did his sister, the princess Alexa.

Her steps slowed as she came up to the terrace; she

found herself approaching the evening with both dread and a tiny, treacherous flicker of anticipation. Sandro's raw, restless energy might disturb her, but it also fascinated her. It was, she knew, a dangerous fascination, and one she needed to get under control if she was going to go ahead with this marriage.

Which she was.

Anything else, at this point, was impossible, involved too much disappointment for too many people.

She forced her worries back along with that fascination as she opened the French windows. As she came inside she stopped short, her breath coming out in a rush, for Alessandro had just emerged from a gilt-panelled door, a frown settled between his dark, straight brows. He glanced up, stilling when he saw her, just as Liana was still.

'Good evening. You've been out for a walk in the gardens?'

She nodded, her mind seeming to have snagged on the sight of him, his rumpled hair, his silvery eyes, his impossibly hard jaw. 'Yes, Your Highness.'

'You're cold.' To her complete shock Alessandro touched her cheek with his fingertips. The touch was so very slight and yet so much more than she'd expected or ever known. Instinctively she jerked back, and she watched as his mouth, which had been curving into a faint smile, thinned into a hard line.

'I'll see you at dinner,' he said flatly. He turned away and strode down the hall.

Drawing a deep breath, she threw back her shoulders, forced herself to turn towards her own suite of rooms and walk with a firm step even as inside she wondered just what would happen tonight—and how she would handle it.

CHAPTER TWO

ALESSANDRO GAZED DISPASSIONATELY at his reflection as he twitched his black tie into place. This afternoon's meeting with Lady Liana had gone about as well as he could have expected, and yet it still left him dissatisfied. Restless, as everything about his royal life did.

This palace held too many painful memories, too many hard lessons. *Don't trust. Don't love. Don't believe that anyone loves you back.*

Every one drilled into him over years of neglect, indifference, and anger.

Sighing, he thrust the thought aside. He might hate returning to the palace, but he'd done it of his own free will. Returned to face his father and take up his kingship because he'd known it was the right thing to do. It was his duty.

And because you, ever naive, thought your father might actually forgive you. Finally love you.

What a blind fool he was.

He wouldn't, Sandro thought as he fastened his cufflinks, be blind about his wife. He knew exactly what he was getting into, just what he was getting from the lovely Lady Liana.

Yet for a moment, when he'd seen Liana coming through the French windows, her hair streaming over her shoulders like pale satin, the fading sunlight touching it with gold, he'd felt his heart lighten rather ridiculously.

She'd looked so different from the coldly composed woman he'd encountered in the formal receiving room. She'd looked alive and vibrant and beautiful, her lavender eyes sparkling, her cheeks pink from the wind.

He'd felt a leap of hope then that she might not be the cold, ambitious queen-in-waiting she'd seemed just hours ago, but then he'd seen that icy self-possession enter her eyes, she'd jerked back when he had, unthinkingly, touched her, and disappointment had settled in him once more, a leaden weight.

It was too late to wish for something else for his marriage, Sandro knew. For his life. When he'd received the phone call from his father—after fifteen years of stony silence on both sides—he'd given up his right to strive or even wish for anything different. He'd been living for himself, freely, selfishly, for too long already. He'd always known, even if he'd acted as if he hadn't, that it couldn't last. Shouldn't.

And so he'd returned and taken up his kingship and all it required…such as a wife. An ambitious, appropriate, perfect wife.

His expression hardening, he turned from his reflection and went in search of the woman who fitted all those soulless requirements.

He found her already waiting in the private dining room he'd requested be prepared for their meal. She stood by the window, straight and proud, dressed in an evening gown of champagne-coloured silk.

Her face went blank as she caught sight of him, and after a second's pause she nodded regally as he closed the door behind him.

Sandro let his gaze sweep over her; the dress was by

no means immodest and yet it still clung to her slight curves. It had a vaguely Grecian style, with pearl-and-diamond clips at each shoulder and a matching pearl-and-diamond pendant nestled in the V between her breasts.

The dress clung to those small yet shapely breasts, nipping in at her waist before swirling out around her legs and ending in a silken puddle at her feet. She looked both innocent and made of ivory, everything about her so cold and perfect, making Sandro want to add a streak of colour to her cheeks or her lips—would her cheeks turn pink as they'd been before if he touched her again?

What if he kissed her?

Was she aware of his thoughts? Did she feel that sudden tension inside her as well? He couldn't tell anything from her blank face, her veiled eyes.

She'd pulled her hair back in a tight coil, emphasising her high cheekbones and delicate bone structure, and he had a mad impulse to jerk the diamond-tipped pins from her hair and see it spill over her shoulders in all of its moon-coloured glory. What would she do, he wondered, if he acted on that urge? How would this ice princess in all her white, silken haughtiness respond if he pulled her into his arms and kissed her quite senseless?

Almost as if she could sense the nature of his thoughts she lifted her chin, her eyes sparking violet challenge. *Good.* Sandro wanted to see emotion crack that icy demeanour; he wanted to sense something real from her, whether it was uncertainty or nervousness, humour or passion.

Passion.

It had been a while since he'd been with a woman, a lot longer since he'd been in a relationship. He felt a kick of lust and was glad for it. Perhaps he would act on it tonight. Perhaps *that* would melt the ice, and he would

find the real woman underneath all that haughtiness…
if she existed at all. He hoped, for both of their sakes,
that she did.

'Did you have a pleasant afternoon?' he asked politely.
He moved to the table that was set for two in front of the
huge fireplace and took the bottle of wine that had been
left open to breathe on the side.

'Yes, thank you.' She remained by the window, utterly
still, watching him.

Sandro lifted the bottle. 'May I pour you a glass?'

A hesitation, and then she nodded. 'Yes, thank you.'

Yes, thank you. He wondered if he could get her to say
it a third time. The woman had perfect manners, perfect
everything, but he didn't want perfection. He wanted
something real and raw and passionate—something he'd
never had with any woman, any *person*, even though he'd
long been looking for it. Searching and striving for it. He
suspected Lady Liana was the last person who could satisfy him in that regard.

He poured them both glasses of red wine, the ruby
liquid glinting in the dancing light thrown from the
flames of the fire. He crossed the room to where she
still stood by the window and handed her the glass, let-
ting his fingers brush hers.

He felt her awareness of that little act, her eyes widening slightly before she took the glass with a murmured
thanks. So far they'd been alone for five minutes and
she'd said thank you three times, and nothing else.

He walked back to the fire, taking a long swallow of
his wine, enjoying the way the velvety liquid coated his
throat and fired his belly. Needing that warmth. 'What
did you think of the gardens? Were they to your liking?'
he asked, turning around to face her. She held the wine

glass in front of her, both hands clasped around it, although she had yet to take a sip.

'Yes, thank you—'

'Yes, thank you,' he mimicked, a sneering, almost cruel tone to his voice. He was reacting out of a deep-seated revulsion to this kind of shallow conversation, this *fakery*. It reminded him of too much disappointment, too much pain. Too many lies. 'Do you say anything else?'

She blinked, but otherwise showed no discomfiture. 'Are you irritated by my manners, Your Highness?'

'You are meant to call me Sandro, but you have yet to do so.'

'I apologise. Your first name does not come easily to me.'

He arched an eyebrow, curious yet also still filled with that edgy restlessness that he knew would lead him to say—or do—things they both might regret.

'And why is that?' he asked, and she lifted her shoulders in a tiny shrug.

'You are the king of Maldinia.'

'It's nothing more than a title.'

Her mouth tightened, eyes flashing before she carefully ironed out her expression, her face smoothing like a blank piece of paper. 'Is that what you truly think?'

No, it wasn't. The crown upon his head—the title before his name—was a leaden weight inside him, dragging him down. It always had been, rife with expectations and disappointment. He'd seen how his father had treated that title, and he had no desire to emulate him. No desire to spiral down that destructive path, and yet he did not know if he possessed the strength to do otherwise. 'What do you think?' he asked.

'I think it is an honour and a privilege.'

'And one you are eager to share.' He heard the sardonic

edge to his words and he knew she did too, even though her expression didn't change, didn't even flicker. Funny, how he knew. How he'd somehow become attuned to this ice princess without even trying.

Or maybe he just knew her type, the kind of woman who would do anything to be queen, who didn't care about love or friendship or any softer emotion. Hadn't he encountered such women before, starting with his own mother? And Teresa had been the same, interested only in his wealth and status. He'd yet to find a woman who didn't care about such things, and he no longer had the freedom to search.

'Of course,' she answered calmly.

'Even though you don't know me.'

She hesitated, and he took another sip of wine, watching her over the rim of his glass. He wondered how far he would have to push her to evoke some response—*any* response. Further than that, clearly, for she didn't answer, merely sipped her own wine, her expression coolly serene.

'It doesn't bother you,' he pressed, 'that we barely know each other? That you are going to pledge your life to a stranger? Your body?'

Awareness flared in her eyes at his provocative remark, and he took a step towards her. He wanted her to admit it did, longed for her to say something real, something about how strange or uncertain or fearful this arrangement was. Something. Anything.

She regarded him for a moment, her expression thoughtful and yet still so shuttered. 'So you asked me earlier,' she remarked. 'And yet I thought that was the point of this evening. To get to know one another.'

'Yet you came to Maldinia prepared to marry me without such a luxury.'

'A fact which seems to provoke you, yet I assume you have been prepared to marry me under the same circumstances?' She was as coolly challenging as he had been, and he felt a flicker of respect, a frisson of interest. At least she'd stopped with her milky thank yous. At least she was being honest, even if he despised such truth.

'I was and still am,' he answered. 'I have a duty to provide an heir.'

The faintest blush touched her cheeks at the mention of heirs and she glanced away. 'So you are acting out of duty, and I am not?'

'What duty insists you marry a king?'

'One it appears you wouldn't understand.'

'Oh, I understand,' he answered, and she pressed her lips together, lifted her chin.

'Do you? Why don't you tell me, then, what you understand?'

He stared at her for a moment, and then decided to answer her with honesty. He doubted he'd get even a flicker of response from her. 'You want a title,' he stated flatly. 'A crown. Wealth and power—'

'And in exchange I will give you my allegiance and service,' she answered back, as unruffled as he'd suspected. 'Children and heirs, God willing. Is it not a fair trade?'

He paused, amazed at her plain speaking, even a little admiring of it. At least she wasn't pretending to him, the way so many others would. He could be thankful for that, at least. 'I suppose it is,' he answered slowly. 'But I would prefer my marriage not to be a trade.'

'And yet it must be, because you are king. That is not my fault.'

'No,' he agreed quietly. 'But even so—'

'You think my reasons for this marriage are less than yours,' Liana finished flatly. 'Less worthy.'

Her astuteness unnerved him. 'I suppose I do. You've admitted what you want, Lady Liana. Money. Power. Fame. Such things seem shallow to me.'

'If I wanted them for my own gratification, I suppose they would be.'

He frowned. 'What else could you possibly want them for?'

She just shook her head. 'What has made you so cynical?'

'Life, Lady Liana. Life.' He glanced away, not wanting to think about what had made him this suspicious, this sure that everyone was just out for something, that people were simply to be manipulated and used. Even your own children.

'In any case, you clearly don't relish the prospect of marriage to me,' she said quietly.

'No, I don't,' he answered after a pause. He turned to meet her clear gaze directly. 'I'm sorry if that offends you.'

'It doesn't offend me,' she answered. 'Surprises me, perhaps.'

'And why is that?'

'Because I had assumed we were in agreement about the nature of this marriage.'

'Which is?' he asked, wanting to hear more despite hating her answers, the reality of their situation.

She blinked, a hint of discomfiture, even uncertainty, in the way she shifted her weight, clutched her wine glass a little more tightly. 'Convenience.'

'Ah, yes. Convenience.' And he supposed it was convenient for her to have a crown. A title. And all the trappings that came with them. 'At least you're honest about it.'

'Why shouldn't I be?'

'Most women who have wanted my title or my money have been a bit more coy about what they really want,' he answered. 'More conniving.'

'You'll find I am neither.'

'How refreshing.'

She simply raised her eyebrows at his caustic tone and Sandro suppressed a sigh. He certainly couldn't fault her honesty. 'Tell me about yourself,' he finally said, and she lifted her shoulders in a tiny shrug.

'What is it you wish to know?'

'Anything. Everything. Where have you been living?'

'In Milan.'

'Ah, yes. Your charity work.'

Ire flashed in her eyes. 'Yes, my charity work.'

'What charity do you support again?'

'Hands To Help.'

'Which is?'

'A foundation that offers support to families with disabled children.'

'What kind of support?'

'Counselling, grants to families in need, practical assistance with the day-to-day.' She spoke confidently, clearly on familiar ground. He saw how her eyes lit up and everything in her suddenly seemed full of energy and determination.

'This charity,' he observed. 'It means a lot to you.'

She nodded, her lips pressed together in a firm line. 'Everything.'

Everything? Her zeal was admirable, yet also surprising, even strange. 'Why is that, Lady Liana?'

She jerked back slightly, as if the question offended her. 'Why shouldn't it?'

'As admirable as it is, I am intrigued. Most people

don't live for their philanthropic causes. I would have thought you simply helped out with various charities as a way to bide your time.'

'Bide my time?'

'Until you married.'

She let out an abrupt laugh, the sound hard and humourless. 'You are as traditional as my parents.'

'Yet you are here.'

'Meaning?'

He spread his hands. 'Not many women, not even the daughters of dukes, would enter a loveless marriage, having barely met the man in question, in this day and age.'

She regarded him coolly. 'Unless, of course, there was something in it for them. Money. Status. A title.'

'Exactly.'

She shook her head. 'And what do you see as being in it for you, Your Highness? I'm curious, considering how reluctant you are to marry.'

His lips curved in a humourless smile. 'Why, all the things you told me, of course. You've detailed your own attributes admirably, Lady Liana. I get a wife who will be the perfect queen. Who will stand by my side and serve my country. And of course, God willing, give me an heir. Preferably two.'

A faint blush touched those porcelain cheeks again, intriguing him. She was twenty-eight years old and yet she blushed like an untouched virgin. Surely she'd had relationships before. Lovers.

And yet in their conversation this afternoon, she'd intimated that she hadn't.

'That still doesn't answer my question,' she said after a moment. 'I understand your need to marry. But why me in particular?'

Sandro shrugged. 'You're a duke's daughter, you have

shown yourself to be philanthropic, your father is an important member of the European Union. You're fertile, I assume?'

The pink in her cheeks deepened. 'There is no reason to think otherwise.'

'I suppose that aspect of unions such as these is always a bit of a risk.'

'And if I couldn't have children?' she asked after a moment. 'Would we divorce?'

Would they? Everything in him railed against that as much as the actual marriage. It was all so expedient, so cold. 'We'll cross that bridge when we come to it.'

'How comforting.'

'I can't pretend to like any of this, Lady Liana. I'd rather have a normal relationship, with a woman who—' He stopped suddenly, realising he was revealing too much. *A woman who chose me. Who loved me for myself, and not because of my money or my crown.* No, he wasn't about to tell this cold-blooded woman any of that.

'A woman who?' she prompted.

'A woman who wasn't interested in my title.'

'Why don't you find one, then?' she asked, and she didn't sound hurt or even peeved, just curious. 'There must be a woman out there who would marry you for your own sake, Your Highness.'

And she clearly wasn't one of them, a fact that he'd known and accepted yet still, when so baldly stated, made him inwardly flinch. 'I have yet to find one,' he answered shortly. 'And you are meant to call me Sandro.'

'Then you must call me Liana.'

'Very well, Liana. It's rather difficult to find a woman who isn't interested in my title. The very fact that I have it attracts the kind of woman who is interested in it.'

'Yet you renounced your inheritance for fifteen years,'

Liana observed. 'Couldn't you have found a woman in California?'

He felt a flash of something close to rage, or perhaps just humiliation. She made it sound as if he was pathetic, unable to find a woman to love him for himself.

And maybe he was—but he didn't like this ice princess knowing about it. Remarking on it.

'The women I met in California were interested in my wealth and status,' he said shortly. He thought of Teresa, then pushed the thought away. He'd tumbled into love with her like a foolish puppy; he wouldn't make that mistake again. He wouldn't have the choice, he acknowledged. His attempt at relationships ended in this room, with this woman, and love had no place in what was between them.

'I'm not interested in your wealth,' Liana said after a moment. 'I have no desire to drape myself with jewels or prance about in designer dresses—or whatever it is these grasping women do.'

There was a surprising hint of humour in her voice, and his interested snagged on it. 'These grasping women?'

'You seem to have met so many, Your— Sandro. I had no idea there were so many cold, ambitious women about, circling like hawks.'

His lips twitched at the image even as a cynical scepticism took its familiar hold. 'So you do not count yourself among the hawks, Liana?'

'I do not, but you might. I am interested in being your queen, Sandro. Not for the wealth or the fame, but for the opportunity it avails me.'

'And what opportunity is that?'

'To promote the charity I've been working for. Hands To Help.'

He stared at her, not bothering to mask his incredulity. Was he really expected to believe such nonsense? 'I know you said that the charity meant everything to you, but, even so, you are willing to marry a complete stranger in order to give it greater visibility?'

She pursed her lips. 'Clearly you find that notion incredible.'

'I do. You are throwing your life away on a good cause.'

'That's what marriage to you will be? Throwing my life away?' She raised her eyebrows, her eyes glinting with violet sparks. 'You don't rate yourself highly, then.'

'I will never love you.' Even if he had once longed for a loving relationship, he knew he would never find it with this woman. Even if she wanted to be queen for the sake of some charity—a notion that still seemed ridiculous— she still wanted to be queen. Wanted his title, not him. Did the reason why really matter?

'I'm not interested in love,' she answered, seeming completely unfazed by his bald statement. 'And since it appears you aren't either, I don't know why our arrangement can't suit us both. You might not want to marry, Your Highness—'

'Sandro.'

'Sandro,' she amended with a brief nod, 'but obviously you have to. I have my own reasons for agreeing to this marriage, as you know. Why can we not come to an amicable arrangement instead of festering with resentment over what neither of us can change?'

'You could change, if you wanted to,' Sandro pointed out. 'As much as you might wish to help this charity of yours, you are not bound by duty in quite the same way as I am.'

Her expression shuttered, and he felt instinctively that

she was hiding something, some secret sorrow. 'No,' she agreed quietly, 'not in quite the same way.'

She held his gaze for a moment that felt suspended, stretching into something else. All of a sudden, with an intensity that caught him by surprise, he felt his body tighten with both awareness and desire. He wanted to know what the shadows in her eyes hid and he wanted to chase them away. He wanted to see them replaced with the light of desire, the blaze of need.

His gaze swept over her elegant form, her slight yet tempting curves draped in champagne-coloured silk, and desire coiled tighter inside him.

An amicable arrangement, indeed. Why not?

She broke the gaze first, taking a sip of wine, and he forced his mind back to more immediate concerns...such as actually getting to know this woman.

'So you live in Milan. Your parents have an apartment there?'

'They do, but I have my own as well.'

'You enjoy city life?'

She shrugged. 'It has proved convenient for my work.'

Her charity work, for which she didn't even get paid. Could she possibly be speaking the truth when she said she was marrying him to promote the charity she supported? It seemed absurd and extreme, yet he had seen the blazing, determined light in her eyes when she spoke of it.

'What has made you so devoted to that particular charity?' he asked and everything in her went tense and still.

'It's a good cause,' she answered after a moment, her expression decidedly wary.

'There are plenty of good causes. What did you say Hands To Help did? Support families with disabled children?'

'Yes.'

A few moments ago she'd been blazing with confidence as she'd spoken about it, but now every word she spoke was offered reluctantly, every movement repressive. She was hiding something, Sandro thought, but he had no idea what it could be.

'And did anything in particular draw you to this charity?' he asked patiently. Getting answers from her now felt akin to drawing blood from a stone.

For a second, no more, she looked conflicted, almost tormented. Her features twisted and her eyes appealed to him with an agony he didn't understand. Then her expression shuttered once more, like a veil being drawn across her face, and she looked away. 'Like I said, it's a good cause.'

And that, Sandro thought bemusedly, was that. Very well. He had plenty of time to discover the secrets his bride-to-be was hiding, should he want to know them. 'And what about before you moved to Milan? You went to university?'

'No. I started working with Hands To Help when I was eighteen.' She shifted restlessly, then pinned a bright smile on her face that Sandro could see straight through.

'What about you, Sandro?' she asked, stumbling only slightly over his name. 'Did you enjoy your university days?'

He thought of those four years at Cambridge, the heady freedom and the bitter disillusionment. Had he enjoyed them? In some respects, yes, but in others he had been too angry and hurt to enjoy anything.

'They served a purpose,' he said after a moment, and she cocked her head.

'Which was?'

'To educate myself.'

'You renounced your title upon your graduation, did you not?'

Tension coiled inside him. That much at least was common knowledge, but he still didn't like talking about it, had no desire for her to dig. They both had secrets, it seemed.

'I did.'

'Why?'

Such a bald question. Who had ever asked him that? No one had dared, and yet this slip of a woman with her violet eyes and carefully blank expression did, and without a tremor. 'It felt necessary at the time.' He spoke repressively, just as she had, and she accepted it, just as he had. Truce.

Yet stupidly, he felt almost disappointed. She wasn't interested in him; of course she wasn't. She'd already said as much. And he didn't want to talk about it, so why did he care?

He didn't. He was just being contrary because even as he accepted the necessity of this marriage, everything in him rebelled against it. Rebelled against entering this prison of a palace, with its hateful memories and endless expectations. Rebelled against marrying a woman he would never love, who would never love him. Would their convenient marriage become as bitter and acrimonious as his parents'? He hoped not, but he didn't know how they would keep themselves from it.

'We should eat,' he said, his voice becoming a bit brusque, and he went to pull out her chair, gesturing for her to come forward.

She did, her dress whispering about her legs as she moved, her head held high, her bearing as straight and proud as always. As she sat down, Sandro breathed in the perfumed scent of her, something subtle and floral, perhaps rosewater.

He glanced down at the back of her neck as she sat, the skin so pale with a sprinkling of fine golden hairs. He had the sudden urge to touch that soft bit of skin, to press his lips to it. He imagined how she would react and his mouth curved in a mocking smile. He wondered again if the ice princess was ice all the way through. He would, he decided, find out before too long. Perhaps they could enjoy that aspect of their marriage, if nothing else.

'What have you been doing in California?' she asked as one of the palace staff came in with their first course, plates of mussels nestled in their shells and steamed in white wine and butter.

'I ran my own IT firm.'

'Did you enjoy it?'

'Very much so.'

'Yet you gave it up to return to Maldinia.'

It had been the most agonising decision he'd ever made, and yet it had been no decision at all. 'I did,' he answered shortly.

She cocked her head, her lavender gaze sweeping thoughtfully over him. 'Are you glad you did?'

'Glad doesn't come into it,' he replied. 'It was simply what I needed to do.'

'Your duty.'

'Yes.'

Sandro pried a mussel from its shell and ate the succulent meat, draining the shell of its juices. Liana, he noticed, had not touched her meal; her mouth was drawn into a prim little line. He arched an eyebrow.

'Are mussels not to your liking?'

'They're delicious, I'm sure.' With dainty precision she pierced a mussel with her fork and attempted, delicately, to wrest it from its shell. Sandro watched, amused, as she wrangled with the mussel and failed. This was a food that required greasy fingers and smacking lips, a wholehearted and messy commitment to the endeavour. He sat back in his chair and waited to see what his bride-to-be would do next.

She took a deep breath, pressed her lips together, and tried again. She stabbed the mussel a bit harder this time, and then pulled her fork back. The utensil came away empty and the mussel flew across her plate, the shell clattering against the porcelain. Sandro's lips twitched.

Liana glanced up, her eyes narrowing. 'You're laughing at me.'

'You need to hold the mussel with your fingers,' he explained, leaning forward, his mouth curving into a mocking smile. 'And that means you might actually get them dirty.'

Her gaze was all cool challenge. 'Or you could provide a knife.'

'But this is so much more interesting.' He took another mussel, holding the shell between his fingers, and prised the meat from inside, then slurped the juice and tossed the empty shell into a bowl provided for that purpose. 'See?' He lounged back in his chair, licking his fingers with deliberate relish. He enjoyed discomfiting Liana. He'd enjoy seeing her getting her fingers dirty and her mouth smeared with butter even more, actually living life inside of merely observing it, but he trusted she would find a way to eat her dinner without putting a single hair out of place. That was the kind of woman she was.

Liana didn't respond, just watched him in that chilly way of hers, as if he was a specimen she was meant to examine. And what conclusions would she draw? He doubted whether she could understand what drove him, just as he found her so impossibly cold and distant. They were simply too far apart in their experience of and desire for life to ever see eye to eye on anything, even a plate of mussels.

'Do you think you'll manage any of them?' he asked, nodding towards her still-full plate, and her mouth firmed.

Without replying she reached down and held one shell with the tips of her fingers, stabbing the meat with her fork. With some effort she managed to wrench the mussel from its shell and put it in her mouth, chewing resolutely. She left the juice.

'Is that what we call compromise?' Sandro asked softly and she lifted her chin.

'I call it necessity.'

'We'll have to employ both in our marriage.'

'As you would in any marriage, I imagine,' she answered evenly, and he acknowledged the point with a terse nod.

Liana laid down her fork; clearly she wasn't going to attempt another mussel. 'What exactly is it you dislike about me, Your Highness?'

'*Sandro.* My name is Sandro.' She didn't respond and he drew a breath, decided for honesty. 'You ask what I dislike about you? Very well. The fact that you decided on this marriage without even meeting me—save an unremarkable acquaintance fifteen years ago—tells me everything I need to know about you. And I like none of it.'

'So you have summed me up and dismissed me, all because of one decision I have made? The same decision you have made?'

'I admit it sounds hypocritical, but I had no choice. You did.'

'And did it not occur to you,' she answered back, her voice still so irritatingly calm, 'that any woman you approached regarding this marriage, any woman who accepted, would do so out of similar purpose? Your wife can't win, Sandro, whether it's me or someone else. You are determined to hate your bride, simply because she agreed to marry you.'

Her logic surprised and discomfited him, because he knew she was right. He was acting shamefully, *stupidly*, taking out his frustration on a woman who was only doing what he'd expected and even requested. 'I'm sorry,' he said after a moment. 'I realise I am making this more difficult for both of us, and to no purpose. We must marry.'

'You could choose someone else,' she answered quietly. 'Someone more to your liking.'

He raised an eyebrow, wearily amused. 'Are you suggesting I do?'

'No, but…' She shrugged, spreading her hands. 'I do not wish to be your life sentence.'

'And will I be yours?'

'I have accepted the limitations of this marriage in a way it appears you have not.'

Which made him sound like a hopeless romantic. No, he'd accepted the limitations. He was simply railing against them, which as she'd pointed out was to no purpose. And he'd stop right now.

'Forgive me, Liana. I have been taking out my frustrations on you, and I will not do so any longer. I wish to marry you and no other. You are, as I mentioned before, so very suitable, and I apologise for seeming to hold it against you.' This little speech sounded stiltedly formal, but he did mean it. He'd made his choices. He needed to live with them.

'Apology accepted,' she answered quietly, but with no

real warmth. Could he even blame her? He'd hardly en-
deared himself to her. He wasn't sure he could.

He reached for his wine glass. 'In any case, after the
debacle of my brother's marriage, not to mention my
parents', our country needs the stability of a shock-free
monarchy.'

'Your brother? Prince Leo?'

'You know him?'

'I've met him on several occasions. He's married to
Alyse Barras now.'

'The wedding of the century, apparently. The love
story of the century....' He shook his head, knowing
how his brother must have hated the pretence. 'And it
was all a lie.'

'But they are still together?'

Sandro nodded. 'The irony is, they actually do love
each other. But they didn't fall in love until after their
marriage.'

'So their six-year engagement was—?'

'A sham. And the public isn't likely to forgive that
very easily.'

'It hardly matters, since Leo will no longer be king.'

God, she was cold. 'I suppose not.'

'I only meant,' she clarified, as if she could read his
thoughts, 'that the publicity isn't an issue for them anymore.'

'But it will be for us,' he filled in, 'which is why I have
chosen to be honest about the convenience of our marriage. No one will ever think we're in love.'

'Instead of a fairy tale,' she said, 'we will have a business partnership.'

'I suppose that is as good a way of looking at it as any
other.' Even if the thought of having a marriage like his
parents'—one born of convenience and rooted in little

more than tolerance—made everything in him revolt. If a marriage had no love and perhaps not even any sympathy between the two people involved, how could it not sour? Turn into something despicable and hate-filled?

How could *he* not?

He had no other example.

Taking a deep breath, he pressed a discreet button to summon the wait staff. It was time for the next course. Time to move on. Instead of fighting his fate, like the unhappy, defiant boy he'd once been, he needed to accept it—and that meant deciding just how he could survive a marriage to Lady Liana Aterno.

CHAPTER THREE

LIANA STUDIED SANDRO'S face and wondered what he was thinking. Her husband-to-be was, so far, an unsettling enigma. She didn't understand why everything she did, from being polite to trying to eat mussels without splattering herself with butter, seemed to irritate him, but she knew it did. She saw the way his silvery eyes darkened to storm-grey, his mobile mouth tightening into a firm line.

So he didn't want to marry her. That undeniable truth lodged inside her like a cold, hard stone. She hadn't expected that, but could she really be surprised? He'd spent fifteen years escaping his royal duty. Just because he'd decided finally to honour his commitments didn't mean, as he'd admitted himself, that he relished the prospect.

And yet it was hard not to take his annoyance personally. Not to let it hurt—which was foolish, because this marriage wasn't personal. She didn't want his love or even his affection, but she had, she realised, hoped for agreement. Understanding.

A footman came in and cleared their plates, and Liana was glad to see the last of the mussels. She felt resentment stir inside her at the memory of Sandro's mocking smile. He'd enjoyed seeing her discomfited, would have probably laughed aloud if she'd dropped a mussel in her lap or sent it spinning across the table.

Perhaps she should have dived in and smeared her face and fingers with butter; perhaps he would have liked her better then. But a lifetime of careful, quiet choices had kept her from making a mess of anything, even a plate of mussels. She couldn't change now, not even over something so trivial.

The footman laid their plates down, a main course of lamb garnished with fresh mint.

'At least this shouldn't present you with too much trouble,' Sandro said softly as the door clicked shut. Liana glanced up at him.

She felt irritation flare once more, surprising her, because she usually didn't let herself feel irritated or angry...or anything. Yet this man called feelings up from deep within her, and she didn't even know why or how. She definitely didn't like it. 'You seem to enjoy amusing yourself at my expense.'

'I meant only to tease,' he said quietly. 'I apologise if I've offended you. But you are so very perfect, Lady Liana—and I'd like to see you a little less so.'

Perfect? If only he knew the truth. 'No one is perfect.'

'You come close.'

'That is not, I believe, a compliment.'

His lips twitched, drawing her attention to them. He had such sculpted lips, almost as if they belonged on a statue. She yanked her gaze upwards, but his eyes were no better. Silvery grey and glinting with amusement.

She felt as if a fist had taken hold of her heart, plunged into her belly. Everything quivered, and the sensation was not particularly pleasant. Or perhaps it was *too* pleasant; she felt that same thrill of fascination that had taken hold of her when she'd first met him.

'I would like to see you,' Sandro said, his voice lowering to a husky murmur, 'with your hair cascading over your shoulders. Your lips rosy and parted, your face flushed.'

And as if he could command it by royal decree, she felt herself begin to blush. The image he painted was so suggestive. And it made that fist inside her squeeze her heart once more, made awareness tauten muscles she'd never even known she had.

'Why do you wish to see me like that?' she asked, relieved her voice sounded as calm as always. Almost.

'Because I think you would look even more beautiful then than you already are. You'd look warm and real and alive.'

She drew back, strangely hurt by his words. 'I am quite real already. And alive, thank you very much.'

Sandro's gaze swept over her, assessing, knowing. 'You remind me of a statue.'

A statue? A statue was cold and lifeless, without blood or bone, thought or feeling. And he thought that was what she was?

Wasn't it what she'd been for the past twenty years? The thought was like a hammer blow to the heart. She blinked, tried to keep her face expressionless. Blank, just like the statue he accused her of being. 'Are you trying to be offensive?' she answered, striving to keep her voice mild and not quite managing it.

His honesty shouldn't hurt her, she knew. There was certainly truth in it, and yet… She didn't want to be a statue. Not to this man.

A thought that alarmed her more than anything else.

'Not trying, no,' Sandro answered. 'I suppose it comes naturally.'

'I suppose it does.'

He shook his head slowly. 'Do you ever lose your temper? Shout? Curse?'

'Would you prefer to be marrying a shrew?' she answered evenly and his mouth quirked in a small smile.

'Does anything make you angry?' he asked, and before she could think better of it, she snapped, 'Right now, you do.'

He laughed, a rich chuckle of amusement, the sound spreading over her like chocolate, warming her in a way she didn't even understand. This man was frustrating and even hurting her and yet…

She liked his laugh.

'I am glad for it,' he told her. 'Anger is better than indifference.'

'I have never said I was indifferent.'

'You have shown it in everything you've said or done,' Sandro replied. 'Almost.'

'Almost?'

'You are not quite,' he told her in that murmur of a voice, 'as indifferent as you'd like me to believe—or even to believe yourself.'

She felt her breath bottle in her lungs, catch in her throat. 'I don't know what you mean, Your Highness.'

'Don't you?' He leaned forward, his eyes glinting silver in the candlelight. 'And must I remind you yet again that you are to call me Sandro?'

She felt her blush deepen, every nerve and sinew and sense so agonisingly aware. Feeling this much *hurt*. She was angry and scared and, most of all, she wanted him… just as he knew she did. 'I am not inclined,' she told him, her voice shaking, 'to call you by your first name just now, *Your Highness*.'

'I wonder, under what circumstances would you call me Sandro?'

Her nails dug into her palms. 'I cannot think of any at the moment.'

Sandro's silvery gaze swept over her in lingering as-
sessment. 'I can think of one or two,' he answered lazily,
and everything in her lurched at the sudden predatory
intentness in his gaze. She felt her heart beat hard in
response, her palms go cold and her mouth dry. 'Yes,
definitely, one or two,' he murmured, and, throwing his
napkin on the table, he rose from the chair.

She looked, Sandro thought, like a trapped rabbit, although perhaps not quite so frightened a creature. Even
in her obvious and wary surprise she clung to her control, to her coldness. He had a fierce urge to strip it away
from her and see what lay beneath it. An urge he intended
to act on now.

Her eyes had widened and she gazed at him unblinkingly, her hands frozen over her plate, the knife and fork
clenched between her slender, white-knuckled fingers.

Sandro moved towards her chair with a loose-
limbed, predatory intent; he was acting on instinct now,
wanting—needing—to strip away her cold haughtiness,
chip away at that damned ice until it shattered all around
them. She would call him Sandro. She would melt in
his arms.

Gently, yet with firm purpose, he uncurled her clenched
fingers from around her cutlery, and the knife and fork
clattered onto her plate. She didn't resist. Her violet gaze
was still fastened on him, her lips slightly parted. Her pulse
thundered under his thumb as he took her by the wrist and
drew her from the chair to stand before him.

Still she didn't resist, not even as he moved closer to
her, nudging his thigh in between her own legs as he
lifted his hands to frame her face.

Her skin was cool and unbearably soft, and he brushed
his thumb over the fullness of her parted lips, heard her

tiny, indrawn grasp, and smiled. He rested his thumb on the soft pad of her lower lip before he slid his hands down to her bare shoulders, her skin like silk under his palms.

He gazed into her eyes, the colour of a bruise, framed by moon-coloured lashes, wide and waiting. Then he bent his head and brushed his mouth across hers, a first kiss that was soft and questioning, and yet she gave no answer.

She remained utterly still, her lips unmoving under his, her hands clenched by her sides. The only movement was the hard beating of her heart that he could feel from where he stood, and Sandro's determination to make her respond crystallised inside him, diamond hard. He deepened the kiss, sliding his tongue into her luscious mouth, the question turning into a demand.

For a woman who was so coldly determined, her mouth tasted incredibly warm and sweet. He wanted more, any sense of purpose be damned, and as he explored the contours of her mouth with his tongue he moved his hands from her shoulders down the silk of her dress to cup the surprising fullness of her breasts. They fitted his hands perfectly, and he brushed his thumbs lightly over the taut peaks. Still she didn't move.

She was like the statue he'd accused her of being, frozen into place, rigid and unyielding. A shaft of both sexual and emotional frustration blazed through him. He wanted—*needed*—her to respond. Physically. Emotionally. He needed something from her, something real and alive, and he would do whatever it took to get it.

Sandro tore his mouth from hers and kissed his way along her jawline, revelling in the silkiness of her skin even as a furious determination took hold of him once more.

Yet as his mouth hovered over the sweet hollow where her jaw met her throat he hesitated, unwilling to continue

when she was so unresponsive despite the insistence pulsing through him. He had never forced a woman, not for
so much as a kiss, and he wasn't about to start now. Not
with his bride. Submission, he thought grimly, was not
the same as acceptance. As want.

Then she let out a little gasping shudder and her hand,
as if of its own accord, clasped his arm, her nails digging
into his skin as she pulled him infinitesimally closer.
She tilted her head back just a little to allow him greater
access to her throat, her breasts, and triumph surged
through him. She wanted this. *Him.*

He moved lower, kissing his way to the V between her
breasts where the diamond-and-pearl pendant nestled.
He lifted the jewel and licked the warm skin underneath,
tasted salt on his tongue and heard her gasp again, her
knees buckling as she sat down hard on the table amidst
the detritus of their dinner.

Triumph mixed with pure lust and he fastened his
hands on her hips, sliding them down to her thighs so
he could spread her legs wider. He stood between them,
the silken folds of her dress whispering around him as
he kissed her like a starving man feasting at a banquet.

He felt her shy response, her tongue touching his before darting away again, and he was utterly enflamed.
He slid the straps of her dress from her shoulders, free-
ing her breasts from their silken prison.

She wore no bra, and desire ripped through him at the
sight of her, her head thrown back, her breath coming in
gasps as she surrendered herself to his touch, her face
flushed and rosy, her lips parted, her body so wonderfully open to him. *This* was how he'd wanted to see her.
He bent his head, kissing his way down her throat, his
hand cupping her bared breast—

And then the door opened and a waitress gasped an

apology before closing it again quickly, but the moment, Sandro knew, had broken. Shattered into shock and awkwardness and regret.

Liana wrenched herself from his grasp, holding her dress up to her bare front, her lips swollen, her eyes huge and dazed as she stared at him.

He stared back in both challenge and desire, because as much as she might want to deny what had just happened between them, her response had said otherwise. Her response had told him she really was alive and warm and real beneath all that ice, and he was glad.

'Don't—' she finally managed, the single word choked, and Sandro arched an eyebrow.

'It's a little late for that. But obviously, I've stopped.'

'You shouldn't have—'

'Stopped?'

'*Started*—'

'And why not? We are to be married, aren't we?'

She just shook her head, fumbling as she attempted to slide her arms back into the dress, but she couldn't manage it without ripping the fragile fabric. Sandro came to stand behind her, unzipping the back with one quick tug.

'*Don't* touch me—'

'I'm helping you dress,' he answered shortly. 'You can't get your arms through the straps otherwise.'

Wordlessly she slid her arms through the straps, and he felt her tremble as he zipped her back up, barely resisting the urge to press his lips to the bared nape of her neck and feel her respond to him again.

Her hair had come undone a bit, a few tousled curls lying against her neck. The back of her dress, he saw, was crumpled and stained from where she'd sat on the table. Just remembering made hot, hard desire surge through him again. She might, for the sake of pride or modesty, play the ice maiden now, but he knew better. He wanted to make her melt again, even as he watched her return to her cold composure, assembling it like armour.

'Thank you,' she muttered and stepped quickly away from him.

'You're welcome.' He surveyed her, noticing the faint pink to her cheeks, the swollen rosiness of her mouth. She would not look at him. 'I'm afraid our meal is quite ruined.'

'I'm not hungry.'

He couldn't resist quipping, 'Not for food, perhaps.'

'Don't.' She dragged her gaze to his, and he was surprised—and slightly discomfited—to see not simple embarrassment in her stormy gaze, but a tortured recrimination that ate at the satisfaction he'd felt at her physical response. He'd seduced her quite ruthlessly, he knew. His kisses and caresses had been a calculated attack against her senses. Her coldness.

But she *had* responded. That had been real. Even if she regretted it now.

He folded his arms. 'Our marriage might be one of convenience, Liana, but that doesn't mean we can't—or shouldn't—desire one another. Frankly I find it a relief.' She shook her head wordlessly, and a different kind of frustration spiked through him. 'What do you see our marriage looking like, then? I need an heir—'

'I *know* that.' She lifted her hands to her hair, fussing with some of the diamond-tipped pins. A few, he saw, had fallen to the floor and silently he bent to scoop them up and then handed them to her. She still wouldn't look at him, just shoved pins into the tangled mass of silvery hair that he now realised was really quite a remarkable colour. Quite beautiful.

'Are you a virgin?' he asked abruptly, and her startled gaze finally met his. She looked almost affronted.

'Of course I am.'

'Of course? You're twenty-eight years old. I'd hardly expect, at that age, for you to save yourself for marriage.'

Colour deepened in her cheeks. 'Well, I did. I'm sorry if that is yet another disappointment for you.' She didn't sound sorry at all, and he almost smiled.

'Hardly a disappointment.' Her response to him hadn't been disappointing at all. 'But I can understand why you might feel awkward or afraid about what happened between—'

'I'm not *afraid*.' Her lips tightened and her eyes flashed. She dropped her hands from her hair and busied herself with straightening her rather ruined dress.

'What, then?' Sandro asked quietly.

Her hands shook briefly before she stilled them, mindlessly smoothing the crumpled silk of her dress. 'I simply wasn't… This isn't…' She took a breath. 'I wasn't expecting this.'

'It should be a happy surprise, then,' Sandro answered. 'At least we desire each other.' She shook her head, the movement violent. 'I still fail to see the problem.'

She drew a breath into her lungs, pressed her hands against her still crumpled dress. 'This marriage was—is—meant to be convenient.'

'Not that convenient,' Sandro answered sharply. 'We were always going to consummate it.'

'I know that!' She took another breath; her cheeks were now bright pink. 'I simply don't… I don't want to *feel*…' She broke off, misery swamping her eyes, her whole body. Sandro had the sudden urge to comfort her, to offer her a hug of affection rather than the calculated caress of moments before.

What on earth was causing her such torment?

Liana felt as if Sandro had taken a hammer to her heart, to her very self, with that kiss. She'd very nearly shattered into a million pieces, and it was only by sheer strength of will that she'd kept herself together.

She'd never been touched like that before, never felt such an overwhelming, aching need for even more. More touches, more kisses, more of Sandro. It had called to a craving inside her she hadn't even known she had. Didn't want.

Because if she opened herself up to wanting anything from Sandro—even *that*—she'd open herself up to pain. To disappointment. To feeling, and she'd cut herself off from all of it for too long to want it now. To risk the fragile security she'd built around her heart, her self.

The point of this marriage, she thought helplessly, was that it wouldn't demand such things of her. It would be safe.

Yet nothing felt safe now. And how could she explain any of it to Sandro without sounding as if she was a freak? A frigid freak?

I'm sorry, Sandro, but I have no desire to enjoy sex with you.

She sounded ridiculous even to herself.

'What is it you don't want to feel, Liana?' he asked and she just stared at him.

This. Him. All of it. What could she tell him? He was clearly waiting for an answer. 'I...I don't want to desire you,' she said, and watched his eyebrows raise, his mouth thin.

'And why is that?'

Because it scares me. You scare me. She'd sound like such a pathetic little mouse, and maybe she was, but she didn't want him knowing it. Knowing how weak and frightened she was, when she'd been trying to seem strong and secure and safe.

Clearly it was nothing more than a facade.

Sandro was still staring at her, his expression narrowed and assessing. He probably couldn't imagine why any woman wouldn't desire him, wouldn't *want* to desire him. She'd read enough gossip websites and trashy tabloids to know Sandro Diomedi, whether he was king of Maldinia or IT billionaire, had plenty of women falling at his feet.

She didn't want to be one of them.

Oh, she'd always known she'd have to do her duty in bed as well as out of it. She might be inexperienced, but she understood that much.

She also knew most people didn't think of it as a duty. She'd read enough novels, seen enough romantic movies to know many people—*most* people—found the physical side of things to be quite pleasurable.

As she just had.

She felt her face heat once more as she remembered how shameless she had been. How good Sandro's mouth had felt on hers, his hands on her body, waking up every deadened nerve and sense inside her—

She looked away from him now, willing the memories to recede. She didn't *want* to wake up. Not like that.

'Liana?' he prompted, and she searched for an answer, something believable. Something that would hurt him, as she'd been hurt first by his derision and incredulity, and then by his desire. A Sandro who reached her with his kiss and caress was far more frightening than one who merely offended her with his scorn.

'Because I don't respect you,' she said, and she felt the electric jolt of shock go through him as if they were connected by a wire.

'Don't *respect*?' He looked shocked, almost winded, and Liana felt a vicious stab of petty satisfaction. He'd shaken up everything inside her, her sense of security and even her sense of self. Let him be the one to look and feel shaken.

Then his expression veiled and he pursed his lips. 'Why don't you respect me?'

'You've shirked your duty for fifteen years, and you need to ask that?'

Colour touched his cheekbones, and she knew she'd touched a nerve, one she hadn't even considered before. But there was truth in what she'd said, what she'd felt. He'd walked away from all he was meant to do, while she'd spent a lifetime trying to earn back her parents' respect for one moment's terrible lapse.

'I didn't realise you were so concerned about my duty.'

'I'm not, but then neither are you,' Liana snapped, amazed at the words—the feeling—coming out of her mouth. Who was this woman who lost her temper, who melted in a man's arms? She felt like a stranger to herself, and she couldn't believe how reckless she'd been with this man…in so many ways. How much he made her feel. Physically. Emotionally. So in the space of a single evening she'd said and done things she never had allowed herself to before.

'You're very honest,' Sandro said softly, his voice a dangerous drawl. 'I appreciate that, if not the sentiment.'

Liana dropped her hand from her mouth, where it had flown at his response. She knew she should apologise, yet somehow she could not find the words, or even the emotion. She wasn't sorry. This man had humiliated and hurt her, used her to prove some terrible point. She might be appallingly innocent by his standards, but she had enough sense to know he'd kissed her not out of simple and straightforward desire, but to prove something. To exhibit his power over her.

And he had. Oh, he had.

But he wouldn't now.

Sandro drew himself up, his mouth as thin and sharp as a blade, his eyes no more than silver slits. 'Clearly we have no more to say to one another.'

'What—?' Shock cut off her voice. Twenty years of trying to be an obedient and dutiful daughter, and she'd wrecked it in a matter of moments. *Why* had she been so impetuous, so stupid?

'I don't think we have any need to see each other again either,' he said, and Liana scrambled to think of something to say, anything to redeem the situation.

'I realise I spoke in haste—'

'And in truth.' He gave an unpleasant smile. 'Trust me, Lady Liana, I do appreciate your honesty. I have lived with far too much dissembling to do otherwise. However, since this is, as we have both agreed, a marriage of convenience, there is no point in attempting to get to know one another or find even one point of sympathy between us. In this case...' he paused, eyeing her coldly '...we will both do our duty.'

Her stomach hollowed out. 'You mean—'

'The wedding will be in six weeks. I'll see you then.' And without another word, the king turned on his heel and left her alone in the room, amidst the scattered dishes and ruined meal, her mind spinning.

Sandro strode from the dining room, fury beating in his blood, his bride-to-be's words ringing in his ears.

You've shirked your duty for fifteen years, and you need to ask that?

She'd cut to the heart of it, hadn't she? The empty heart of him. And even though he knew she was right, it was exactly what he had done, and he hated that she knew. That she'd pointed it out, and that she didn't respect him because of it. Who was she but a woman intent on selling herself for a crown and a title, never mind how she cloaked it with ideas of duty and selfless charity work? How dared she toss her contempt of him in his face?

And yet still her words cut deep, carved themselves into his soul. They held up a mirror to the selfishness of his heart, the inadequacy he felt now, and he couldn't stand it. Couldn't stand the guilt that rushed through him, along with the resentment. He didn't want to be here, didn't want to be king, didn't want any of this, and yet it was his by right. By duty. Even if he didn't deserve it. Even if he felt afraid—*terrified*—that he could not bear the weight of the crown his father hadn't even wanted to give him.

He yanked open the door to the study that had once been his father's and still smelled of his Havana cigars. Sandro opened a window and breathed in the cold night air, tinged even here in the city with the resin of the pines that fringed the capital city. He willed his heart to slow, the remnants of his desire, making his body ache with unfulfilment, to fade.

Briefly he considered whether he should break off his engagement. Find another bride, someone with a little more warmth, a little more heart. Someone who might actually respect him.

And just who would that be, when the truth is and always will be that you walked away from your duty?

That you don't deserve your crown or the respect it commands?

He closed his eyes briefly, pictured his father's face twisted in derision moments before he'd died.

You think I wanted this? You?

And deluded fool that he insisted on being, he actually had. Had hoped, finally, that his father accepted him. Loved him.

Idiot.

Sandro let out a shuddering breath and turned away from the window. He wouldn't call off the wedding, wouldn't try to find a better bride. He was getting about as good a deal as he could hope for.

What kind of woman, after all, agreed to a marriage of convenience? A woman like Liana, like his mother, intent on everything but emotion. And that was fine, really, because he didn't have the energy for emotion either. He didn't even think he believed in love anymore, so why bother searching for it? Wanting it?

Except that need seemed hardwired into his system, and had been ever since he'd been a little boy, desperate for his father's attention, approval, and most of all, love, when all he'd wanted was to use him as a pawn for publicity, so he could pursue his own selfish desires. Desires Sandro had been blinded to until his naive beliefs had been ripped away.

'Sandro?'

Sandro turned around to see his brother, Leo, standing in the doorway of his study. Six months ago Leo had been first in line to the throne, as he had been ever since their father had disinherited Sandro and put Leo forward. Fifteen years of bracing himself for the crown, and then Sandro had unexpectedly returned and set him free. At least that was how Sandro had always viewed it; Leo hadn't protested, and Sandro knew his brother hated the pretence of royal life as much as he had.

Yet he'd made a damn good heir to the throne in his absence, so much so that Sandro had wondered if Leo regretted his return.

He'd chosen not to ask.

Leo was a cabinet minister now, lived in a town house in Averne with his bride Alyse, and was working on passing a bill to provide broadband to the entire country, drag Maldinia into the twenty-first century.

'What is it?' Sandro heard the terse snap of his voice and sighed, rubbing a hand over his face. 'Sorry. It's been a long day.'

'You met with Lady Liana?'

'Yes.'

'Is she suitable?'

Sandro laughed, the sound humourless and harsh. 'Definitely.'

Leo stepped into the room and closed the door. 'You don't sound pleased.'

'Did either of us really wish to marry for duty?'

'Sometimes it can work out,' Leo answered, a hint of a smile in his voice, on his face.

'Sometimes,' Sandro agreed. Things had certainly worked out for his brother. He was in love with his wife and free to pursue his own interests and ambitions as he chose.

'I always thought Liana was nice enough,' Leo offered carefully. 'Although she seemed…sad to me, sometimes.'

'Sad?' Sandro shook his head even as he recalled the shadows in her eyes, the secrets he felt she'd been hiding. Yes, she had seemed sad. She'd also seemed determined, resolute, and as cold and hard as the diamond she'd worn around her neck. The diamond he'd lifted when he'd licked the skin underneath....

Remembering made lust beat along with his fury, and hell if that wasn't an unwholesome mix. Sighing, he pushed away from the window. 'I didn't realise you knew her.'

Leo's smile was wry. 'Father considered an alliance between us, briefly.'

'An alliance? You mean *marriage*?' Sandro turned around to stare at his brother in surprise. Yet how could he really be shocked? Leo had been the future king. And hadn't Liana already shown him just how much she wanted to be queen? For fifteen years—over half her life—he'd been essentially out of the picture. Of course she'd looked at other options.

As had his own brother, his own father.

'So what happened?' he asked Leo, and his brother's smile was crooked and yet clearly full of happiness. Of joy.

'Alyse happened.'

Of course. Sandro had seen the iconic photo himself, when it had been taken over six years ago. Leo had been twenty-four, Alyse eighteen. A single, simple kiss that had rocked the world and changed their lives for ever. And for the better now, thank God.

'Although to be honest,' Leo continued, 'I don't think Liana was ever really interested. It seemed as if she was humouring me, or maybe her parents, who wanted the match.'

Or hedging her bets, perhaps, Sandro thought, just in case the black-sheep heir made a reappearance. 'I'm happy for you, you know,' he said abruptly. 'For you and Alyse.'

'I know you are.'

Yet he heard a coolness in his brother's voice, and he could guess at its source. For fifteen years they hadn't spoken, seen each other, or been in touch in even the paltriest of ways. And this after their childhood, when they'd banded together, two young boys who had had only each other for companionship.

Sandro knew he needed to say something of all that had gone before—and all that hadn't. The silence and separation that had endured for so long was, he knew, his fault. He was the older brother, and the one who had left. Yet the words he knew he should say burned in his chest and tangled in his throat. He couldn't get them out. He didn't know how.

This was what happened when you grew up in a family that had never shown love or emotion or anything real at all. You didn't know how to be real yourself, as much as you craved it—and you feared that which you craved.

And yet Leo had found love. He was real with Alyse. Why, Sandro wondered in frustration, couldn't he be the same?

And in the leaden weight of his heart he knew the answer. Because he was king…and he had a duty that precluded such things.

CHAPTER FOUR

LIANA GAZED AT her reflection in the gold-framed mirror of one of the royal palace's many guest suites. She was in a different one from the last time she'd been here six weeks ago, yet it was just as sumptuous. Then she'd come to Maldinia to discuss marriage; this time she was here for a wedding. Hers.

'You're too thin.' Her mother Gabriella's voice came out sharp with anxiety as she entered the room, closing the door behind her.

'I have lost a little weight in the past few weeks,' Liana said, and heard the instinctive note of apology in her voice. Everything with her parents felt like an apology, a way to say sorry over and over again. Yet she could never say it enough, and her parents never seemed to hear it anyway.

They certainly never talked about it.

'I suppose things have been a bit stressful,' Gabriella allowed. She twitched Liana's short veil over her shoulders and smoothed the satin fabric of the simple white sheath dress she wore.

Her wedding to Sandro was to be a quiet affair in the palace's private chapel, with only family in attendance. After the fairy-tale proportions of Leo and Alyse's ceremony, and the resulting fallout, something quiet and dignified was needed. It suited Liana fine.

She wondered what Sandro thought about it. She hadn't seen him since she'd arrived two days ago, beyond a formal dinner where she'd been introduced to a variety of diplomats and dignitaries. She'd chatted with everyone, curtsied to the queen, who had eyed her coldly, and met Sandro's sister, Alexa, as well as his brother, Leo, and sister-in-law, Alyse.

Everyone—save the queen—had been friendly enough, but it had been Sandro's rather stony silence that had unnerved her. It had occurred to her then in an entirely new and unwelcome way that this man was going to be her *husband*. She would live with him for the rest of her days, bear his children, serve by his side. Stupid of her not to think it all through before, but suddenly it seemed overwhelming, her decision reckless. Was she really going to say vows based on a desire to please her parents? To somehow atone for the past?

No wonder Sandro had been incredulous. And it was too late to change her mind now.

Gabriella put her hands on Liana's shoulders, met her gaze in the mirror. 'You do want this marriage, Liana, don't you?' Liana opened her mouth to say of course she did, because she knew she couldn't say anything else. Not when her mother wanted it so much. Even now, with all the doubts swirling through her mind, she felt that. Believed it.

'Because I know we might seem old-fashioned to you,' Gabriella continued in a rush. 'Asking you to marry a man you've barely met.' Now Liana closed her mouth. It was old-fashioned, but she wasn't going to fight it. Wasn't going to wish for something else.

What was the point? Her parents wanted it, and it was

too late anyway. And in any case, a real marriage, a marriage based on intimacy and love, held no appeal for her.

Neither did a husband who seemed as if he hated her.

And wasn't that her fault? For telling him she didn't respect him? For pushing him away out of her own hurt pride and fear? But perhaps it was better for Sandro to hate her than call up all those feelings and needs. Perhaps antipathy would actually be easier.

'I just want you to be happy,' Gabriella said quietly. 'As your father does.'

And they thought marrying a stranger would make her happy?

No, Liana thought tiredly, they didn't want her to be happy, not really. They wanted to feel as if she had been taken care of, dealt with. Tidied away. They wanted to forget her, because she knew soul deep that every time her parents looked at her they were reminded of Chiara. Of Chiara's death.

Just as she was.

If she married Sandro, at least she'd be out of the way. Easier to forget.

Better for everyone, really.

She drew a breath into her lungs, forced her expression into a smile. 'I am happy, Mother. I will be.'

Her mother nodded, not questioning that statement. Not wanting to know. 'Good,' she said, and kissed Liana's cold cheek.

A few minutes later her mother left for the chapel, leaving Liana alone to face the walk down the aisle by herself. Maldinian tradition dictated that the bride walk by herself, and the groom keep his back to her until she reached his side.

A stupid tradition, probably meant to terrify brides into submission, she thought with a grimace. And would it terrify her? What would the expression on Sandro's face be when he did turn around? Contempt? Disgust? Hatred? *Desire?* She knew she shouldn't even care, but she did.

Ever since she'd first met Sandro, she'd started caring. Feeling. And that alarmed her more than anything.

She closed her eyes, fought against the nerves churning in her stomach and threatening to revolt up her throat. Why had this man woken something inside her she'd thought was not just asleep, but dead? How had he resurrected it?

She longed to go back to the numb safety she'd lived in for so long. For twenty years, since she was eight. Eight years old, pale faced and trembling, staring at the grief-stricken expressions on her parents' faces as she told them the truth.

I was there. It was my fault.

And they had, in their silence, agreed. Of course they had, because it *was* the truth. Chiara's death had been entirely her fault, and that was a truth she could never, ever escape.

This marriage was, in its own way, meant to be more penance. But it wasn't meant to make her *feel*. Want. Need.

Yet in the six weeks since she'd returned from Maldinia, it had. She felt the shift inside herself, an inexorable moving of the tectonic plates of her soul, and it was one she didn't welcome. Ever since Sandro's scathing indictment of her, his assault on her convictions, her body, her whole self, she'd started to feel more. Want more. And she was desperate to stop, to snatch back the numbness, the safety.

'Lady Liana? It's time.'

Woodenly Liana nodded and then followed Paula, the

palace's press secretary, to the small chapel where the service would take place.

'This will be a very quiet affair,' Paula said. 'No cameras or publicity, like before.'

Before, when Alyse and Leo's charade had blown up in their faces, Liana knew, and they'd been exposed as having faked their fairy-tale love story for the entirety of their engagement. This time there was no charade, yet Liana still felt as if everything could explode around her. As if it already had.

'All right, then.' Paula touched her briefly on her shoulder. 'You look lovely. Don't forget to smile.'

Somehow Liana managed to make the corners of her mouth turn up. Paula didn't look all that satisfied by this expression of expectant marital joy, but she nodded and left Liana alone to face the double doors that led to the chapel, the small crowd, and Sandro.

Drawing a deep breath, she straightened her shoulders, lifted her chin. She was doing this for a good reason. Forget her own feelings, which she'd tried to forget for so long anyway. There was a good reason, the best reason, to marry Sandro, to make her life worth something. Her sister.

For a second, no more, she allowed herself to think of Chiara. *Chi-Chi.* Her button eyes, her impish smile, her sudden laugh.

I'm doing this for you, Chi-Chi, she thought, and tears, tears she hadn't let herself cry for twenty years, rose in her eyes. She blinked them back furiously.

Forward.

'Lady Liana?'

Liana turned to see Alyse Barras—now Diomedi— walking towards her, a warm smile on her pretty face. She wore an understated dress of rose silk, with a matching coat and hat. Silk gloves reached up to the elbow on each slender arm. She looked every inch the elegant, confident royal.

Liana had met Alyse briefly at the dinner last night, but they hadn't spoken beyond a few pleasantries.

'I'm sorry we haven't had a chance to talk properly,' Alyse said, extending one hand that Liana took stiffly, still conscious of the tears crowding under her lids. 'I just wanted to tell you I know how you feel. Walking down an aisle alone can be a little frightening. A little lonely.' Her gaze swept over Liana's pale figure in obvious sympathy, and she instinctively stiffened, afraid those treacherous tears would spill right over. If they did, she feared there would be no coming back from it.

'Thank you,' she said, and she knew her voice sounded too cool. It was her only defence against losing it completely in this moment. 'I'm sure I'll manage.'

Alyse blinked, her mouth turning down slightly before she nodded. 'Of course you will. I just wanted to say... I hope we have a chance to get to know one another now that we're both part of this family.' Her smile returned. 'For better or for worse.'

And right now felt like worse. Liana nodded, too wretchedly emotional to respond any further to Alyse's friendly overture.

'Thank you,' she finally managed. 'I should go.'

'Of course.' Alyse nodded and stepped back. 'Of course.'

Two footmen came forward to throw open the doors of the chapel, and with that icy numbness now hastily re-assembled, her chin lifted and her head held high, Liana stepped into her future.

The chapel was as quiet and sombre as if a funeral were taking place rather than a wedding. A handful of guests she didn't know, her parents in the left front row. Sandro's back, broad and resolute, turned towards her. She felt the tears sting her eyes again, her throat tighten and she willed the emotion away.

This was the right thing to do. The only thing she could do. This was her duty to her parents, to the memory of her sister. She was doing it for them, not for herself. *For Chiara....*

She repeated the words inside her head, a desperate chant, an appeal to everything she'd done and been in the twenty years since Chiara's death.

This was her duty. Her atonement. Her absolution. She had no other choice, no other need but to serve her parents and the memory of her sister as best she could.

And as she came down the aisle she finally made herself believe it once more.

Sandro had heard the doors to the chapel open, knew Liana was walking towards him. He fought an urge to turn around, knowing that tradition had Maldinian grooms—royal ones, at least—facing the front until the bride was at their side.

When she was halfway down he gave in and turned around, tradition be damned. He wanted to see Liana, wanted to catch a glimpse of the woman he was about to promise to love, honour, and cherish before he made those binding vows. For the past six weeks he'd been trying *not* to think of her, of the proud contempt he'd seen on her face the last time they'd spoken, when she'd told him with a sneer in her voice that she didn't respect him.

And as shocked as her contemptuous indictment had been, how could he actually be surprised? Hurt? She'd been speaking the truth, after all.

Now as she came down the aisle, her bearing regal

and straight, her chin tilted proudly and her eyes flashing violet ice, he felt the hopes he hadn't even realised he still had plummet.

She was just as he remembered. Just as composed, just as soulless and scornful as he'd first feared. And in about three minutes she would become his wife.

As she joined him at the altar, her dress whispering against his legs, she lifted her chin another notch, all haughty pride and cool purpose.

Sandro turned away without so much as a smile and listened to the archbishop begin with a leaden heart.

An hour later they were man and wife, circulating through one of the palace's many receiving rooms among the few dozen guests. They still hadn't spoken to each other, although Sandro had brushed his lips against Liana's cold ones at the end of the ceremony before she'd stepped quickly away.

They'd walked down the aisle together, her hand lying rigidly on his arm, and gone directly to one of the palace's salons for a champagne reception.

Liana, Sandro couldn't help notice, seemed to take to the role of queen with instant, icy poise. She smiled and chatted with a reserved dignity that he supposed fitted her station. She was friendly without being gregarious or warm or real.

She wasn't, he thought, anything he wanted. But he had to live with it, with her, and he was determined to put such thoughts behind him.

He moved through the crowds, chatting with various people, conscious of Liana by his side, smiling and yet so still and straight, so proud. She seemed untouchable and completely indifferent to him, yet even so he found his mind—and other parts of his body—leaping ahead to a few hours from now, when they would leave the reception and all the guests behind and retire upstairs to the tower room that was the traditional honeymoon suite.

There wouldn't actually be a honeymoon; he saw no point, and he doubted Liana did either. But tonight... Tonight they would consummate their marriage. The prospect filled him with desire and distaste, hunger and loathing.

He wanted her, he knew, but he didn't want to want her, not when she didn't even respect him. And she obviously didn't want to want him.

Sandro took a long swallow of champagne, and it tasted bitter in his mouth. What a mess.

Liana felt tension thrum through her body as she made a valiant effort to listen to another dignitary talk about Maldinia's growing industry, and how Prince Leo was helping to raise funds for technological improvements.

But her real focus was on the man next to her. Her husband. He listened and chatted and smiled just as she did, but she felt the tension in his body, had seen the chilly expression in his eyes when he'd turned to her, and in the moment before she'd said her vows she had felt panic bubble up inside her. She'd wanted to rip off her veil and run back down the aisle, away from everything. The anxiety and hope in her parents' eyes. The ice in her groom's. And the churning fear and guilt inside herself that she could never escape, no matter how far or fast she ran.

And so she'd stayed and repeated the vows that would bind her to this man for life. She'd promised to love and honour and obey him, traditional vows for a traditional marriage, and she'd wished she'd considered how different it would feel, to fill her mouth full of lies.

She didn't love this man. She hadn't honoured him. And as for obedience...

Sandro placed a hand on her elbow, and despite every intention not to feel anything for him, just that simple touch set sparks racing up her arm, exploding in her heart. She hated how much he affected her. Hated how weak and vulnerable he made her feel, how he made her want things she knew he would never give her.

'We will say our goodbyes in a few minutes,' he said in a low voice, and Liana stiffened.

'Goodbyes? But we're not going anywhere.'

Sandro's mouth curved in a humourless smile. His eyes were as hard as metal. 'We're going to our honeymoon suite, Liana. To go to bed.'

She pulled her arm away from his light touch, realisation icing her veins. Of course. Their wedding night. They would have to consummate their marriage now. It was a duty she'd known she would have to perform, even if she hadn't let herself think too much about it. Now it loomed large and incredibly immediate, incredibly *intimate*, and even as dread pooled in her stomach she couldn't keep a contrary excitement from leaping low in her belly—fear and fascination, desire and dread all mixed together. She hated the maelstrom this man created within her.

'You aren't going to steal away yet, are you?' Alyse approached them, Leo by her side. 'I haven't even had a chance to talk with Liana yet, not properly.'

Liana offered a sick smile, her mind still on the night ahead, alone with Sandro.

'You'll have plenty of opportunity later,' Sandro answered, his fingers closing once more over Liana's elbow. 'But for now I want my bride to myself.' He smiled as he said it, but to Liana it felt like the smile of a predator, intent on devouring its prey.

And that was how intimacy with Sandro felt. Like

being devoured. Like losing herself, everything she'd ever clung to.

Alyse glanced uncertainly at Sandro before turning back to Liana. 'We'll have to have a proper chat soon,' she said, and Liana nodded jerkily.

'Yes, I look forward to getting to know both of you,' she said with as much warmth as she could inject into her voice, although she feared it wasn't all that much. 'You both seem very happy in your marriage.'

'And you will be in yours, Queen Liana,' Leo said quietly, 'if you just give Sandro some time to get used to the idea.'

Liana watched as he slipped his hand into his wife's, his fingers squeezing hers gently. Something in her ached at the sight of that small yet meaningful touch. When had she last been touched like that?

It had been years. Decades. She'd found it so hard to give and receive affection after Chiara's death. For a second she could almost feel her sister's skinny arms hook around her neck as she pressed her cheek next to hers. She could feel her silky hair, her warm breath as she whispered in her ear. She'd always had secrets, Chiara, silly secrets. She'd whisper her nonsense in Liana's ear and then giggle, squeezing her tight.

Liana swallowed and looked away. She couldn't think of Chiara now or she'd fall apart completely. And she didn't want to think about the yearning that had opened up inside her, an overwhelming desire for the kind of intimacy she'd closed herself off from for so long. To give and receive. To know and be known. To love and be loved.

None of it possible, not with this man. Her husband.

She might be leaving this room for her wedding night, but that kind of intimacy, with love as its sure foundation, was not something she was about to experience. Something she didn't *want* to experience, even if everything in her protested otherwise.

Love opened you up to all sorts of pain. It *hurt*.

But she didn't even need to worry about that, because right now she and Sandro were just going to have sex. Emotionless sex.

They spent the next few minutes saying their goodbyes; her mother hugged her tightly and whispered that she hoped she would be happy. Liana murmured back nonsense about how she already was and saw the tension that bracketed her mother's eyes lessen just a little. Her father didn't hug her; he never had, not since Chiara had died. She didn't blame him.

A quarter of an hour later she left the reception with Sandro; neither of them spoke as they walked down several long, opulent corridors and then up the wide front staircase of the palace, down another corridor, up another staircase, and finally to the turret room that was kept for newlyweds.

Sandro opened the door first, ushering her in, and Liana didn't look at him as she walked into the room. She took in the huge stone fireplace, the windows open to the early evening sky, the enormous four-poster bed piled high with silken pillows and seeming almost to pulse with expectation.

She resisted the urge to wipe her damp palms against the narrow skirt of her wedding gown and walked to the window instead, taking in several needed lungfuls of mountain air. The sun was just starting to sink behind the timbered houses of Averne's Old Town, the Alps fringing the horizon, their snowy peaks thrusting towards a violet sky. It was all incredibly beautiful, and yet also chilly and remote. As chilly and remote as she felt, shrinking further and further into herself, away from the reality—the intimacy—of what was about to happen between them.

Behind her she heard the door click shut.

'Would you like to change?' Sandro asked. He sounded formal and surprisingly polite. Liana didn't turn from the window.

'I don't believe I have anything to change into.'

'There's a nightdress on the bed.'

She turned then and saw the silk-and-lace confection spread out on the coverlet. It looked horribly revealing, ridiculously romantic. 'I don't see much point in that.'

Sandro huffed a hard laugh. 'I didn't think you would.'

She finally forced herself to look at him. 'There's no point in pretending, is there?'

'Is that what it would be?' He lounged against the doorway; while she'd been gazing out of the window he'd shed his formal coat and undone his white tie. His hair was ruffled, his eyes sleepy, and she could see the dark glint of a five o'clock shadow on his chiselled jaw, the hint of chest hair from the top opened buttons of his shirt. He looked dissolute and dangerous and...*sexy*.

The word popped into her head of its own accord. She didn't want to think of her husband as sexy. She didn't want to feel that irresistible magnetic pull towards him that already had her swaying slightly where she stood. She didn't want to feel so *much*. If she felt this, she'd feel so much more. She would drown in all the feelings she'd suppressed for so long.

'You weren't pretending the last time I kissed you,' Sandro said softly, and to Liana it sounded like a taunt.

'You're as proud as a polecat about that,' she answered. Sandro began to stroll towards her.

'Why fight me, Liana? Why resist me? We're married. We must consummate our marriage. Why don't we at least let this aspect of our union bring us pleasure?'

'Because nothing else about it will?' she filled in, her tone sharp, and Sandro just shrugged.

'We've both admitted as much, haven't we?'

Yes, she supposed they had, so there was no reason for her to feel so insulted. So *hurt*. Yet as Sandro kept moving towards her with a predator's prowl, she knew she did.

He stopped in front of her, close enough so she could feel the heat of him, and he could see her tremble. She stared blindly ahead, unable to look at him, to see what emotion flickered in his eyes. Pity? Contempt? Desire? She wanted none of it, even as her body still ached and yearned.

Sandro lifted one hand and laid it on her shoulder; she could feel the warmth of his palm from underneath the thin silk of her gown. He smoothed his hand down the length of her arm, the movement studied, almost clinical, as if he was touching a statue. And she felt like a statue just as he'd accused her of being: lifeless, unmoving, even as her blood heated and her heart lurched. Sandro sighed.

'Why don't you take a bath?' he said, turning away. 'Relax for a little while. If you don't want to wear that nightgown, there are robes in the bathroom that will cover you from chin to toe.'

She watched out of the corner of her eye as he moved to the fireplace, his fingers deftly undoing the remaining studs of his shirt. He shrugged out of it, the firelight burnishing the bronzed skin of his sculpted shoulders, and Liana yanked her gaze away.

On shaky, jelly-like legs she walked to the bathroom, her dress whispering around her as she moved, and closed the door. Locked it. And let out a shuddering breath that ended on something halfway to a sob.

CHAPTER FIVE

SANDRO LEANED BACK in the chair by the fire and gazed moodily at the flames flickering in the huge hearth. Resentment warred with guilt inside him as he listened to Liana move in the bathroom, turning on taps. Taking off her clothes. Would she be able to get that slinky dress off by herself? He knew she wouldn't ask for help.

Ever since they'd entered this room with all of its sensual expectation she'd become icier than ever. It angered him, her purposeful coldness, as if she couldn't stand even to be near him and wanted him to know it, but he still couldn't keep a small stab of pity from piercing his resentment. She was a virgin; even if she would never admit it, she had to be a little nervous. He needed to make allowances.

The desire he'd felt for her still coiled low in his belly but even so he didn't relish the prospect of making love to his wife. Of course there would be no love about it, which was neither new nor a surprise. He shouldn't even want it, not when he knew what kind of woman Liana really was.

He had no illusions about how she would handle their wedding night. Lie stiff and straight as a board on that sumptuous bed, scrunch her eyes tight, and think of her marital duty. Just the thought of it—of her like that—was enough to turn his flickering desire into ash.

Distantly Sandro realised the sounds from the bathroom had stopped, and he knew she must be stuck in that dress. He rose from the chair, dressed only in his trousers, and rapped on the bathroom door.

'Liana? Do you need help getting out of your gown?' Silence. He almost smiled, imagining how she was wrestling with admitting she did, and yet not wanting to accept anything from him. Certainly not wanting him to unzip her. 'I'll close my eyes,' he said dryly, half joking, 'if you want me to help you unzip it.'

'It's not a zipper.' Her voice sounded muffled, subdued. 'It's about a hundred tiny buttons.'

And before he could stop himself, Sandro was envisioning all those little buttons following the elegant length of her spine, picturing his fingers popping them open one by one and revealing the ivory skin of her back underneath. Desire leapt to life once more.

'Then you most certainly need help,' he said, and after a second's pause he heard the sound of the door unlocking and she opened it, her head bowed, a few tendrils of hair falling forward and hiding her face.

Wordlessly she turned around and presented him with her narrow, rigid back, the buttons going from her neck to her tailbone, each one a tiny pearl.

Sandro didn't speak as he started at the top and began to unbutton the gown. The buttons were tiny, and it wasn't easy. It wasn't a matter of a moment either, and he didn't close his eyes as he undid each one, the tender skin of her neck and shoulders appearing slowly underneath his fingers as the silk fell away in a sensual slide.

His fingers brushed her skin—she felt both icy and soft—and he felt her give a tiny shudder, although whether she was reacting out of desire or disgust he didn't know. He sensed she felt both, that she was as conflicted as he was—probably more—about wanting him. The realisation sent a sudden shaft of sympathy through him and he stilled, his fingers splayed on her bared back. He felt her stiffen beneath him.

'If you'd rather,' he said softly, 'we can wait.'

'Wait?' Her voice was no more than a breath, her back still rigid, her head bowed.

'To consummate our marriage.'

'Until when?'

'Until we're both more comfortable with each other.'

She let out a little huff of laughter, the sound as cynical as anything he'd ever heard. 'And when will that be, do you think, Your Highness? I'd rather just get it over with.'

What a delightful turn of phrase, he thought sardonically. Her skin had warmed under his palm but when he spread his fingers a little wider he felt how cold she still was. Cold all the way through. 'You're right, of course,' he answered flatly. 'We might as well get it over with.'

She didn't answer, and he finished unbuttoning the dress in silence. She held her hands up to her front to keep it in place, and Sandro could see the top curve of her bottom, encased enticingly in sheer tights, as she stepped back into the bathroom. She closed the door, and with a grim smile he listened to her lock it once more.

Liana lay in the bath until the water grew cold and the insistent throb of her body's response to Sandro started to subside—except it didn't.

She'd never been touched so intimately as when he'd unbuttoned her dress. She realised this probably made her seem pathetic to a man like him, a man who was so sensual and passionate, who had probably had a dozen—a hundred—lovers. As for her? She'd had so little physical affection in her life that even a casual brush of a hand had everything in her jolting with shocked awareness.

And now the feeling of his fingers on her back, the whisper of skin on skin, so intimate, so *tender*, an assault so much softer and gentler than that life-altering kiss they'd had six weeks ago and yet still so unbearably powerful, had made that awakened need inside her blaze hotter, harder, its demand one she was afraid she could not ignore.

The water was chilly now, and reluctantly she rose from the tub, and swathed herself in the robe that covered her just as Sandro had promised but which she knew he could peel away in seconds.

She took time brushing and blow-drying her hair, stared at her pale face and wide eyes, and then pinched her cheeks for colour. No more reasons to stay in here, to stall.

Taking a deep breath, she opened the bathroom door.

Sandro was facing the window, one arm braced against its frame, wearing only a pair of black silk pyjama bottoms, and the breath rushed from Liana's lungs as she gazed at him, the firelight flickering over his powerful shoulders and trim hips, his hair as dark as ink and his skin like bronze. He looked darkly powerful and almost frightening in his latent sensuality, his blatant masculinity. Just his presence seemed to steal all the breath from her body, all the thoughts from her head.

She straightened her spine, took a deep breath. 'I'm ready.'

'Are you?' His voice was a low, sardonic drawl as he turned around, swept her from head to toe in one swiftly assessing gaze. 'You look terrified.'

'Well, I can't say I'm looking forward to this,' Liana

answered, keeping her voice tart even though her words were, at least in part, no more than lies. 'But I'll do my duty.'

'I thought you'd say something like that.'

'Then perhaps you're getting to know me, after all.'

'Unfortunately, I think I am.'

She flinched, unable to keep herself from it, and Sandro shook his head. 'I'm sorry. That was uncalled for.'

'But you meant it.'

'I only meant…' He let out a long, low breath. 'I just wish things could be different.'

That she was different, he meant. Well, sometimes she wished she were different too. She wished being close to someone—being vulnerable, intimate, *exposed*—wasn't scary. Terrifying.

Was that what Sandro wanted? That kind of…closeness? The thought caused a blaze of yearning to set her senses afire. Because part of her wanted that too, but she had no idea how to go about it. How to overcome her fear.

'Well, then,' she finally said, every muscle tensed and expectant. A smile twitched at his lips even though she still sensed that restless, rangy energy from him.

'Do you actually think I'm going to pounce on you right this second? Deflower you like some debauched lord and his maiden?'

'I hope you'll have a bit more finesse than that.'

'Thank you for that vote of confidence.' He strolled towards her with graceful, loose-limbed purpose that had Liana tensing all the more.

He stood in front of her, his gaze sweeping over her so that already she felt ridiculously exposed, even though she wore the bathrobe that covered her completely.

'You're as tense as a bow.' Sandro touched the back

of her neck, his fingers massaging the muscles knotted there. 'Why don't you relax, just a little?'

Her fingers clenched convulsively on the sash of her robe. Relaxation felt like an impossibility. 'And how am I supposed to do that when I know—' She stopped abruptly, not wanting to admit so much, or really anything at all.

Sandro's dark eyebrows drew together in a frown as he searched her face. 'When you know what?'

'That you don't like me,' she forced out, her voice small and suffocated, her face averted from his. 'That you don't even respect me or hold me in any regard at all.'

Sandro didn't answer, just let his gaze rove over her, searching for something he didn't seem to find because he finally sighed, shrugged his powerful shoulders. 'And you feel the same way about me.'

'I—' She stopped, licked her lips. She should tell him that she'd only told him she didn't respect him to hurt him and hide herself, because she'd hated how vulnerable she'd felt. And yet somehow the words wouldn't come.

'I think it's best,' Sandro said quietly, 'if we put our personal feelings aside. The last time we were alone together, I kissed you.' He spoke calmly, rationally, and yet just that simple statement of fact caused Liana's heart to thud even harder and a treacherous, hectic flush to spread over her whole body. 'You responded,' he continued, and she closed her eyes, the memory of his kiss washing over her in a hot tide. 'And I responded to you. Regardless of how different we are, and how little regard we have for each other's personal priorities or convictions, we are physically attracted to one another, Liana.'

He rested his hands lightly on her shoulders, and she felt the warmth of his palms even through the thick terry cloth of her robe. 'It might seem repellent to you, to be attracted to someone you don't respect, but *this* is the only point of sympathy it appears we have between us.'

And with his hands still on her shoulders he bent his head and brushed his lips across hers. That first taste of him was like a cool drink of water in the middle of a burning desert. And her life *had* been a desert, a barren wasteland of loneliness and yearning for something she hadn't realised she'd missed until he'd first touched her.

Her mouth opened instinctively under his, her hands coming up to clutch the warm, bare skin of his shoulders, needing the contact and the comfort, the closeness. Needing him.

His lips hovered over hers for a moment, almost as if he was surprised by the suddenness of her response, the silent *yes* she couldn't keep her body from saying. Then he deepened the kiss, his tongue sweeping into the softness of her mouth, claiming and exploring her with a staggering intimacy that felt strangely, unbearably sweet.

It felt *important*, to be touched like this. To feel warm hands on her body, gentle, caressing, accepting her in a way she'd never felt accepted before. Not since she'd lost Chiara, since she'd let her go.

She'd never understood how much she needed this in the years since then, the touch of a human being, the reminder that she was real and alive, flesh and blood and bone, emotion and want and need. She was so much more than what she'd ever let herself be, and she felt it all now in an overwhelming, endless rush as Sandro kissed her.

And then he stopped, pulling back just a little to smile down at her with what seemed terribly like smugness. 'Well, then,' he said softly, and she heard satisfaction and perhaps even triumph in his voice, and with humiliation scorching through her she pulled away.

Of course he didn't accept her. Didn't like her, didn't

respect her. Didn't even know her. And she didn't want him to, not really, so with all that between them, how could she respond to him this way? How could she crave the exposing intimacy she hated and feared?

Numbness was so much easier. So much safer. She might have lived her life in a vacuum, but at least it had been safe.

She tried to pull back from Sandro's light grasp and he frowned.

'What's wrong?'

'I don't—'

'Want to want me?' he filled in, his voice hardening, and Liana didn't answer, just focused on keeping some last shred of control, of dignity, intact. *Blink. Breathe. Don't cry.*

'But you do want me, Liana,' Sandro said softly. 'You want me very much. And even if you try to deny it, I'll know. I'll feel your response in your lips that open to mine, in your hands that reach for me, in your body that responds to me.' He brushed his hand against her breast, his thumb finding the revealingly taut peak even underneath her heavy robe. 'You see? I'll always know.'

'I know that,' she choked. 'I'm not denying anything.' She turned her face with all of its naked emotion away from him.

'No,' he agreed, his voice as hard as iron now, as hard as his gunmetal-grey eyes. 'You're not denying it. You're just resisting it with every fibre of your being. Resisting me.' She let out a shudder, and he shook his head. 'Why, Liana? You agreed to this marriage, as I did. Why can't we find this pleasurable at least?'

'Because…' Because she wasn't strong enough. She'd open herself up to him just a little and a tidal wave of emotion would rush through her. She wouldn't be able to hold it back and it would devastate her. She knew it instinctively, knew that giving in just a little to Sandro would crack her right open, shatter her into pieces. She'd never come together again.

How could she explain all of that?

And yet even so, she knew she had to stop fighting him, stop this futile resistance, because what purpose did it really serve? She was married to this man. She had known they would consummate this marriage. She just hadn't expected to feel so much.

'Liana,' Sandro said, and he sounded so tired. Weary of this, of her.

'I'm sorry,' she said quietly. 'I'll…I'll try better.'

'Try better?' He raised his eyebrows. 'You don't need to prove yourself to me, Liana.'

Didn't she? Hadn't she been proving herself to her parents, to everyone, for so long she didn't know how to do anything else? How to just *be*?

She dragged in a deep breath. 'Let's…start over.' She forced herself to meet his narrowed gaze, even to smile although she felt her lips tremble, and the tears she'd kept at bay for so long threatened once more to spill.

When had she become so emotionally fragile? Why did this man call up such feelings in her? She wanted to be strong again. She wanted to be safe.

She wanted to get this awful, exposing encounter over with.

'Start over,' Sandro repeated. 'I'm wondering just how far we need to go back.'

'Not that far.' She made her smile brighter, more determined. She could do this. They'd get over this, and life would be safe again. 'You're right. I…I do want you.' The words were like rocks in her mouth; she nearly choked on them. Willing her hands to be steady, she undid the sash of her robe, shrugged it off, and stood before him naked.

Sandro's gaze widened, and Liana felt herself flush, a rosy stain covering her whole body that could not be hidden. And she longed to hide it, hide her whole self, mind and body and heart, yet she forced herself to stand there, chin tilted proudly, back straight. Proud and yet accepting.

Sandro shook his head, and her heart swooped inside her. 'This isn't starting over,' he said quietly. 'This is you just gritting your teeth a bit more and putting a game face on.'

'No—' she said, and with desperation driving her, a desperate need to get this all finished with so she could hide once more, she crossed to him and, pressing her naked body against his, she kissed him.

Sandro felt the softness of her breasts brush his bare chest, her lips hard and demanding on his, a supplication his libido responded to with instant acceptance. Instinctively his arms came up and he pulled her closer, fitted her against the throb of his arousal and claimed the kiss as his own.

She tasted so sweet, and her body was so soft and pliant against his. Too pliant. He inwardly cursed.

He didn't want this. Liana might be submitting to him, but it was an awful, insulting submission. He wanted her want, needed her not just to acknowledge her desire of him, but to embrace it, *him*, even if just physically. Emotionally they might be poles apart, but couldn't they at least have this?

Almost roughly, his own hands shaking, he pushed her away from him and shook his head.

'No. Not like this.'

Her eyes widened. 'Why not?'

He stared at her for a moment, wondering just what was going on behind that beautiful, blank face. Except she wasn't quite so blank right now. Her eyes were filled with panic, and her breath came in uneven, frantic gasps.

This wasn't the understandable shy reticence of a virgin, or even the haughty acceptance of the ice queen he'd thought she was. This was, he realised with a sudden jolt of shock, pure *fear*.

'Liana…' He put his hands on her shoulders and felt a shudder rack her body. 'Did you have a bad experience?' he asked quietly. 'With a man? Is that why you're afraid of me? Of physical intimacy?'

She whirled away, snatched up her robe, and pushed her arms into the billowing sleeves. 'I'm not afraid.'

'You're certainly giving a good impression, then.' He folded his arms, a cold certainty settling inside him. Something had happened to her. It all made sense: her extreme devotion to her charity work, her lack of relationships, her fear of natural desire. 'Were you…abused? Raped?'

She whirled back round to face him, a look of shocked disbelief on her face. *'No!'*

'Most women wouldn't fight a natural, healthy desire for a man, Liana. A man who has admitted he wants you. Why do you?'

'Because…' She licked her lips. 'Because I wasn't expecting it,' she finally said and he raised his eyebrows.

'You weren't expecting us to find the physical side of things pleasant? Why not?'

She shrugged. 'Nothing about this marriage or our meeting suggested we would.'

'The kiss we shared six weeks ago didn't clue you in?'

he asked, a gentle hint of humour entering his voice, surprising even him.

She blushed. He liked it when she blushed, liked how it lit up her face and her eyes, her whole self. It gave him hope. 'Before that, I mean,' she muttered.

'All right, fine. You weren't expecting it. But now it's here between us, and you're still fighting it. Why?'

She hesitated, her gaze lowered, before she lifted her face and pinned him with a clear, violet stare. 'Because I agreed to this marriage because it was convenient, and I didn't want anything else. I didn't want love or even affection. I didn't want to get to know you beyond a…a friendly kind of agreement. I thought that's how you would think of this marriage too, and so far nothing—' her breath hitched, her face now fiery '—nothing has been like I expected!'

He didn't know whether to laugh or groan. 'But you're still not telling me why you don't want those things,' Sandro finally said quietly. 'Why you don't want love or affection.' And while her admission didn't surprise him, he suspected the reason for it was different from what he'd thought. She wasn't cold. She was hiding.

She stared at him mutinously, and then her lower lip trembled. It made him, suddenly and fiercely, want to take her in his arms and kiss that wobbling lip. Kiss the tears that shimmered in her eyes, tears he knew instinctively she wouldn't let fall. Then the moment passed and her expression became remote once more. 'I just don't.'

'Still not an answer, Liana.'

'Well, it's the only one I have to give you.'

'So you don't want to tell me.'

'Why should I?' she demanded. 'We barely know each other. You don't—'

'Like you?' he filled in. 'That might have been true

initially, but how can I ever get to like you, or even know you, if you hide yourself from me? Because that's what the whole ice-princess act is, isn't it? A way to hide yourself.' He'd never felt more sure of anything. Her coldness was an act, a mask, and he felt more determined than ever to make it slip, to have it drop away completely.

'Oh, this is ridiculous.' She bit her lip and looked away. 'I don't know why you can't just toss me on the bed and have your wicked way with me.'

He let out a choked laugh of disbelief. Liana, it seemed, had read a few romance novels. 'You'd really prefer that?'

'Yes.' Her eyes turned the colour of a stormy sea and she shook her head. 'I want to want that,' she said, her voice filled with frustration, and he thought he understood.

She wanted something different now. Well, so did he. He wanted to know this contrary bride of his, understand her in a way he certainly didn't now. But he was getting a glimpse of the woman underneath the ice, a woman with pain and secrets and a surprising humour and warmth. A woman he could live with, maybe even love.

Unless of course he was being fanciful. Unless he was fooling himself just as he had with Teresa, with his father, believing the best of everyone because he so wanted to love and be loved.

But surely he'd developed a little discernment over the years?

'I'm not going to throw you on that bed, Liana,' he said, 'and have my way with you, wicked or otherwise. When we have sex—and it won't be tonight—it will be pleasurable for both of us. It will involve a level of give and take, of vulnerability and acceptance I don't think you're capable of right now.'

She didn't answer, just flashed those stormy eyes at

him, so Sandro smiled and took a step closer to her. 'But I will sleep with you in that bed. I'll lie next to you and put my arms around you and feel your softness against me. I think that will be enough for tonight.' He watched her eyes widen with alarm. 'More than enough,' he said, and he tugged on the sash of her robe so it fell open and she walked unwillingly towards him.

'What are you doing—?'

'You can't sleep in that bulky thing.' He slid it from her shoulders, smoothing the silk of her skin under his palms. 'But if you want to wear that frothy nightgown, go ahead.'

Her chin jutting out in determination, she yanked the nightgown from the bed and put it on. It was made mostly of lace, clinging to her body, and Sandro's palms itched to touch her again.

'Now what?' she demanded, crossing her arms over her breasts.

'Now to bed,' Sandro said, and he pulled her to the bed, lay down, and drew her into his arms. She went unresistingly, yet he felt the tension in every muscle of her body. She was lying there like a wooden board.

He stroked her hair, her shoulder, her hip, keeping his touch gentle yet sure, staying away from the places he longed to touch. The fullness of her breasts, the juncture of her thighs.

If he was trying to relax her, it wasn't working. Liana quivered under his touch, but it was a quiver of tension rather than desire. Again, Sandro wondered just what had made his wife this way.

And he knew he wanted to find out. It would, he suspected, be a long, patient process.

He continued to slide his fingers along her skin even as his groin ached with unfulfilled desire. He wanted her, wanted her in a way he hadn't let himself before. He'd fought against this marriage, against this woman, because he'd assumed she was the same as the other conniving women he'd known. His mother. Teresa.

But he suspected now—hell, knew—that his wife wasn't like that. There was too much fear and vulnerability in that violet gaze, too much sorrow in her resistance. She fought against feeling because she was afraid, and he wanted to know why. He wanted to know what fears she hid, and he wanted to help her overcome them. He wanted, he realised with a certainty born not of anger or rebellion but of warmth and fledgling affection, to melt his icy wife.

CHAPTER SIX

LIANA STIRRED SLOWLY to wakefulness as morning sunshine poured into the room like liquid gold. It had taken her hours to get to sleep last night, hours of lying tense and angry and afraid, because this was so not what she'd expected from her marriage. What she'd wanted.

Yet it seemed it was what she'd wanted, after all, for with every gentle stroke of Sandro's fingers she felt something in her soften. Yearn. And even though her body still thrummed with tension, the desire to curl into the heat and strength of him, to feel safe in an entirely new way, grew steadily like a flame at her core.

And yet she resisted. She fought, because fear was a powerful thing. And her mind raced, recalling their conversations, Sandro's awful questions.

Were you abused? Raped?

He wasn't even close, and yet she was hiding something. Too many things. Guilt and grief and what felt like the loss of her own soul, all in the matter of a moment when she'd failed to act. When she'd shown just what kind of person she really was. He'd seen that, even if he didn't understand the source, and she could never tell him.

Could she? Could she change that much? She didn't know if she could, or how she would begin. With each stroke of Sandro's fingers she felt the answer. *Slowly. Slowly.*

And eventually she felt her body relax of its own accord, and her breath came out in a slow sigh of surrender. She didn't curl into him or move at all, but she did sleep.

And she woke with Sandro's hand curved round her waist, his fingers splayed across her belly. Nothing sexual about the touch, but it still felt unbearably intimate. She still felt a plunging desire for him to move his hand, higher or lower, it didn't matter which, just *touch* her.

And then Sandro stirred, and everything in her tensed once more. He rose on one elbow, brushed the hair from her eyes, his fingers lingering on her cheek.

'Good morning.'

She nodded, unable to speak past the sudden tightness in her throat. 'Sleep well?' Sandro asked, and she heard that hint of humour in his voice that had surprised her last night. She'd seen this man cold and angry and resentful, but she hadn't seen him smile too much. Had only heard him laugh once.

And when he softened like this, it made her soften too, and she didn't know what would happen then.

'Yes.' She cleared her throat, inched away from him. 'Eventually.'

'I slept remarkably well.' He brushed another tendril of hair away from her cheek, tucked it behind her ear, his fingers lingering.

Liana resisted the urge to lean into that little caress. 'What are we going to do today?'

'We have a few engagements.' Smiling, Sandro sat up in bed, raking his hair with his hands, so even though she was trying to avoid looking at him Liana found her gaze drawn irresistibly to his perfectly sculpted pectoral muscles, the taut curve of his biceps. Her husband was beautiful—and fit.

'What engagements?' she asked, forcing her brain back into gear.

'A brunch with my delightful mother as well as my sister and my brother and his wife. An appearance on the balcony for the adoring crowds.'

He spoke with a cynicism she didn't really understand, although she could probably guess at. 'You don't like being royal,' she said, 'do you?'

He sighed and dropped his hands. 'Not particularly. But hadn't you already figured that out, since I shirked my royal duty for fifteen years?' His gaze met hers then, and instead of anger she saw recrimination. She recognised it, because she'd felt it so often herself.

'I shouldn't have said that,' she said quietly. 'I'm sorry.'

'Why, Liana.' He touched her chin with his fingers, tilting her face so their gazes met once more. 'I don't think you've ever apologised to me before. Not sincerely.'

'I am sorry,' she answered. Her chin tingled where he touched her. 'I was just trying to hurt you, so I said the first thing that came to mind.'

'Well, there was truth in it, wasn't there?' His voice came out bitter and he dropped his hand from her face. 'I did shirk my duty. I ran away.'

And she knew all too well how guilt over a mistake, a wrong choice, ate and ate at you until there was nothing left. Until your only recourse was to cut yourself off from everything because numbness was better than pain. Was that how Sandro felt? Did they actually have something—something so fundamental to their selves—in common?

'But you came back,' she said quietly. 'You've made it better.'

'Trying to.' He threw off the covers and rose from

the bed. 'But we should get ready. We have a full day ahead of us.'

He was pulling away from her, she knew. They'd had a surprising moment of closeness there, a closeness that had intrigued her rather than frightened her. And now it was Sandro was who shuttering his expression, and she felt a frustration that was foreign to her because she was usually the one who was pulling away. Hiding herself.

So maybe this was why Sandro had been feeling so frustrated. It was hard to be on the receiving end of someone's reticence—especially when you actually wanted something else. Something more.

'Where are we meant to get ready?' she asked. 'I've only got my wedding dress or this nightgown here.'

Sandro pushed a discreet button hidden in the woodwork of the wall. 'One of your staff will show you to your room,' he said and turned away.

A few minutes later a shy young woman named Maria came to the honeymoon suite and showed Liana her own bedroom, a room, judging from its frilly, feminine décor, Sandro clearly wouldn't share.

So this was what a marriage of convenience looked like, Liana thought, and wondered why she didn't feel happier. Safer. She'd have her own space. Sandro would leave her alone. All things she'd wanted.

Yet in that moment, standing amidst the fussy little tables and pink canopied bed, she wasn't quite so sure she wanted them anymore. They didn't feel as comforting as she'd expected.

Maybe she was just tired. Feeling more vulnerable from everything she and Sandro had said and shared last night. The memory of his hands gently stroking her from shoulder to thigh still had the power to make her quiver.

Enough. It was time to do the work she'd come here

to do, to be queen. To remember her duty to her parents, to her sister, to everything she'd made her life about.

And not think about Sandro, and the confusion of her marriage.

An hour later she was showered and dressed in a modest dress of lavender silk, high necked and belted at the waist. She'd pulled her hair back into its usual tight chignon and then frowned at her reflection, remembering what Sandro had said.

I would like to see you with your hair cascading over your shoulders. Your lips rosy and parted, your face flushed.

For a second she thought about undoing her hair. Putting some blusher on her cheeks. Then her frown deepened and she turned away from the mirror. She looked fine.

Downstairs, the royal family had assembled in an opulent dining room for the official brunch. And it felt official, far from a family meal. A dozen footmen were stationed around the room, and the dishes were all gold plate.

The queen dowager glided into the room, her eyes narrowed, her mouth pursed, everything about her haughty and distant.

Was that how Sandro saw her? Icy and remote, even arrogant? Liana felt herself inwardly cringe. She'd never considered how others saw her; she'd just not wanted to be seen. Really seen. The woman underneath the ice. The girl still trying to make herself invisible, to apologise for her existence.

Sophia went to the head of the table and Sandro moved to the other end. A footman showed Liana her place, on the side, and for a second she hesitated.

As queen, her place was where Sophia now sat, eyeing everyone coldly. Clearly the queen dowager did not want to give up her rights and privileges as monarch, and Liana wasn't about to make a fuss about where she sat at the table. She never made a fuss.

And yet somehow it hurt, because she realised she wanted Sandro to notice where she sat. Notice her, and put her in her rightful place.

He didn't even look at her, and Liana didn't think she was imagining the triumph glittering in her mother-in-law's eyes as she sat down.

Sandro excused himself directly after the brunch, and Liana hadn't had so much as two words of conversation with him. They were meant to appear on the palace balcony at four o'clock, and she had a meeting with her secretary—someone already appointed and whom she hadn't met—at three.

And until then? She'd wander around the palace and wonder yet again just what she was doing here. What had brought her to this place.

Most of the palace's ground floor was made up of formal receiving rooms much like the one she'd first met Sandro in. Liana wandered through them, sunlight dappling the marble floors. As she stood in the centre of one room, feeling as lost and lonely as she ever had and annoyed that she did, she heard a voice from behind her.

'Hello.'

She turned to see Alyse standing in the doorway, looking lovely and vibrant and full of purpose. She'd changed from her more formal outfit for brunch, and now wore a pair of jeans and a cashmere sweater in bright pink. Liana suddenly felt absurd and matronly in her high-necked dress and tightly coiled hair. She fiddled with the pearls at her throat, managed a smile.

'Hello.'

'Did you have a good night?' A blush touched Alyse's cheeks. 'Sorry. I didn't mean that— Well.' She laughed and stepped into the room. 'I was only asking if you'd slept well.'

'Very well, thank you,' Liana answered automatically, and Alyse cocked her head.

'You look tired,' she said, her voice filled with sympathy. 'It's so overwhelming, isn't it—marrying into royalty?'

'It's been a lot to take in,' Liana answered carefully. She didn't want to admit just how overwhelming it had been, and how uncertain and unfulfilled she felt now.

'At least you don't have the press to deal with,' Alyse said with a little laugh. 'That was the hardest part for me. All those cameras, all those reporters looking for a hole in our story, and of course they found one.'

'Was that very hard?'

Alyse made a face. 'Well, I certainly didn't like facing down all those sneering reporters, but the hardest part was how it affected Leo and me.'

Curious now, Liana took an inadvertent step towards her sister-in-law. 'And how did it?'

'Not well. Everything was so fragile between us then. It wasn't ready to be tested in such a way.' She gave Liana a smile. 'Fortunately we survived it.'

'And you love each other now.' Alyse's smile was radiant, the joy in her voice audible, and Liana felt a sharp shaft of jealousy. She'd never wanted what Alyse and Leo had before, never let herself want it. Yet now the yearning that had been skirting her soul seemed to swamp it completely.

She swallowed past the huge lump that had formed in her throat and forced a smile. 'I'm so happy for you.' And she was, even if she was also jealous. Even if she was realising she wanted something more than she could ever expect from Sandro, or even herself.

'It might not be for me to say this,' Alyse said quietly, laying a hand on Liana's arm, 'but Leo and Sandro—they haven't had easy lives, royal though they may be.'

'What do you mean?'

'Their relationship with their parents…' Alyse sighed and shook her head. 'It wasn't healthy or loving. Far from it.'

Liana just nodded. She couldn't exactly say her relationship with her parents was healthy, even if she loved them. She wasn't sure if they loved her. If they could, anymore, and she could hardly blame them.

'Sophia doesn't seem like the most cuddly person I've ever met,' she said, and Alyse gave a wry smile back.

'No, and neither was the king. And yet I think both Leo and Sandro wanted their love, even if they wouldn't admit it. They might not trust love, they might even be afraid of it, but they want it.'

'Leo did,' Liana corrected.

'And I think Sandro does too. Give him a chance, Liana. That's all I'm really saying.'

And again Liana could just nod. Sandro might want love, but he didn't want *her* love. Did he? Or could he change? Could *she*?

She still didn't know if she wanted to change, much less whether she had the courage to try. She'd entered this marriage for a lot of reasons, and none of them had been love. She'd never even let herself think about love.

She'd been skating on the surface of her life, and now the ice below was starting to crack—and what was beneath it? What would happen when it shattered and she fell? She couldn't bear to find out, and yet she had a horrible feeling she would whether she wanted to or not.

But would Sandro be there to catch her? Would he even want to?

'Thank you for telling me all this,' she said, turning back to Alyse. 'It's very helpful.'

'Of course. And you must come have dinner with us one night, you and Sandro. Escape from the palace for a bit.'

After Alyse had gone she went to meet her private secretary, an efficient young woman named Christina. Liana sat and listened while Christina outlined all her potential engagements: cutting ribbons at openings of hospitals and schools, attending events and galas, choosing a wardrobe created by Maldinian fashion designers.

'Are there many?' she asked. 'Maldinia is a small country, after all.'

'A few,' Christina said confidently. 'But of course, your stylist will go over that with you.'

'All right.' Already Liana felt overwhelmed. She hadn't considered any of this. 'I'd like to support a charity I've been working with for many years,' she began, and Christina nodded quickly.

'Of course, Hands To Help. Perhaps a fundraiser in the palace?'

'Oh, yes, that would be wonderful.' She felt her heart lighten at the thought. 'I can contact them—'

'I believe they've already been contacted by King Alessandro,' Christina said. 'It was his idea.'

'It…was?' Liana blinked in surprise. Sandro had seemed sceptical and even mystified about her charity work, yet he'd thought to arrange a fundraiser? Her heart lightened all the more, so it felt like a balloon on a string, soaring straight up. 'Where is the king? Do you know?'

Christina glanced at her watch. 'I imagine he's getting ready for your appearance together in twenty minutes.'

She pulled out a pager and pressed a few numbers. 'I'll page your stylist.'

Just minutes later Liana was primped and made up for the appearance on the balcony. Sandro strode into the room, looking as handsome as ever in his royal dress, but also hassled. Liana's heart, so light moments ago, began a free fall. She hated that her mood might hinge on his look, that such a small thing—the lack of a greeting or a glance—could affect it.

And yet it did. Despite all her attempts to remain removed, remote, here she was, yearning. Disappointed.

'Ready?' he said, barely looking at her, and then with his hand on her lower back they stepped out onto the ornate balcony overlooking the palace courtyard, now filled with joyous Maldinians.

The cheer that rose from the crowd reverberated right through her, made her blink in surprise. She'd never felt so much...*approval*.

'I think they want us to kiss,' Sandro murmured, and belatedly Liana realised they were chanting *'Baccialo!'*

Sandro slid his hand along her jaw, turned her to face him. His fingers wrapped around the nape of her neck, warm and sure, as he drew her unresistingly towards him. His lips brushed hers, soft, hard, warm, cool—she felt it all in that moment as her head fell back and her hands came up to press against his chest.

The roar of the crowd thundered in her ears, matching her galloping pulse as Sandro's mouth moved over hers and everything inside her cracked open.

She wanted to be kissed like this. Loved like this. She was tired of hiding away, of staying safe.

Sandro stepped away with a smile. 'That ought to do it.'

Liana blinked the world back into focus and felt everything in her that had cracked open scuttle for shelter. That kiss had been for the crowds, not for her. It hadn't meant anything.

Their marriage was still as convenient as it ever had been…and she wished it weren't.

As soon as they left the balcony Sandro disappeared again and Liana went to meet with her stylist and go over her wardrobe choices.

'A queen should have a certain modest style,' the stylist explained as she flipped through pages of designs, 'but also be contemporary. The public should feel you can relate to them.'

Liana glanced down at her chaste, high-necked dress. 'So what I'm wearing…?'

'Is beautiful,' the stylist, Demi, said quickly. 'So elegant and classic. But perhaps something a little…fresher?'

'Yes, I suppose I could update my look a little bit,' Liana said slowly. She'd been dressing, for the most part, like a businesswoman facing menopause, not a young woman in her twenties. A young woman with everything ahead of her.

But she'd never actually felt as if she had anything ahead of her before, and she didn't know if she did now.

She had a quiet supper in her bedroom, as Sophia was dining out and Alyse and Leo had gone back to their town house. Sandro was working through dinner, and it wasn't until it was coming on ten o'clock that she finally went to find him.

She had no idea what she'd say, what she wanted to say. He was leaving her alone, just as she'd hoped and wanted. How could she tell him she actually wanted something different now, especially when she wasn't sure herself what that was?

She wandered through the downstairs, directed by footmen to his private study in the back of the palace. With nerves fluttering in her tummy and her heart starting to thud, she knocked on the door.

'Come in.'

Liana pushed open the door and stepped into a wood-panelled room with deep leather club chairs and a huge mahogany desk. Sandro sat behind it, one hand driven through his hair as he glanced up from the papers scattered on his desk.

'Liana—' Surprise flared silver in his eyes and he straightened, dropping his hand. 'I'm sorry. It's late. I've been trying to clear my desk but it never seems to happen.'

'A king has a lot of work to do, I suppose,' she answered with a small smile. Sandro might have avoided his royal duty for most of his adult life, but he was certainly attending to it now.

'What have you been doing today? You had some appointments?'

She nodded. 'With my private secretary and stylist. I've never had a staff before.'

'And is it to your liking?'

'I don't know whether it is or not. It's overwhelming, I suppose. My style is meant to be fresher, apparently.'

'Fresher? It makes you sound like a lettuce.'

'It does, doesn't it?' She smiled, enjoying this little banter. 'I know I've dressed a bit—conservatively.'

He glanced at the lavender dress she still wore. 'And why do you think that is?'

'I suppose I've never wanted to draw attention to myself.'

He nodded slowly, accepting, and Liana fiddled with

the belt at her waist, uncomfortable with even this little honesty. 'Are you—are you coming to bed?'

He gazed at her seriously. 'Do you want me to?'

Yes. And no. She didn't know what she wanted anymore. She'd had such clear purpose in her life...until now. Until she suddenly wanted more, more of him, more of feeling, more of life. Yet she couldn't articulate all that now to Sandro.

He sat back, his hands laced over his middle as he let his gaze sweep over her. 'You're still scared. Of me.'

'Not of you—'

'Of marriage. Of—intimacy.'

She swallowed hard, the sound audible. 'Yes.' It was more than she'd ever admitted before.

'Well, you can breathe easy, Liana. We won't make love tonight.'

Make love. And didn't that conjure all sorts of images in her head? Images that made her dizzy, desires that dried her throat and made everything inside her ache. 'When—?' she asked, her voice only a little shaky, and he smiled.

'Soon, I think. Perhaps on our honeymoon.'

'Honeymoon?' They weren't meant to have a honeymoon. What was the point, when your marriage was about convenience?

'Well, honeymoon might be overstating it a bit. I have to go to California, wrap up some business. I want you to go with me.'

Her cheeks warmed, her blood heated. Everything inside her melted. *He wanted her.* Was it foolish to feel so gratified? So...thrilled?

'Is that all right?' Sandro asked quietly. 'Do you want to go with me, Liana?'

A week ago, a day ago, she would have prevaricated.

Protected herself. She'd never admitted want to herself, much less to another person. Now she nodded. 'Yes,' she said. 'I want to go with you.'

CHAPTER SEVEN

SANDRO SAT ACROSS from Liana on the royal jet and picked a strawberry dipped in chocolate from the silver platter between them. He held it out to her, a mischievous smile playing about his mouth. They were halfway across the Atlantic and he was determined to begin what he suspected would be the very enjoyable process of melting his wife.

It was already working; last night she'd lain in his arms and it had only taken her an hour to relax. He'd watched her face soften in sleep, those tightly pursed lips part on a sigh. Her lashes had fluttered and brushed against her porcelain-pale cheeks. He'd stroked her cheek, amazed at its softness, at the softness he felt in himself towards this woman he'd thought was so hard. So icy and cold.

Yet even as he'd held her and stroked her cheek, he'd wondered. Doubted, because God only knew his judgment had been off before. He'd thought the best of his parents, of the one woman he'd let into his heart. He'd insisted on it, even when everything said otherwise.

Was he doing the same now? Desperate, even now, to love and be loved? Because Liana might lie in his arms, but she didn't always look as if she wanted to be there. One minute she was kissing him with a sudden, sweet passion that had taken him by surprise on the balcony and the next she was cool and remote, all chilly indifference.

Which was the real woman?

Now Liana eyed the chocolate strawberry askance. 'You have a thing about messy food.'

'They tend to be aphrodisiacal.'

'Aphro— *Oh.*' Her cheeks pinked, and he grinned.

'Try one.'

'I don't—'

'You don't like strawberries? Or chocolate? I can't believe it.'

'I've never had one before.'

'A strawberry?'

'Not one dipped in chocolate.' Her blush deepened and she looked away. 'Sometimes I think I must seem ridiculous to you.'

Surprise made him falter. He dropped his hand, still holding the strawberry, the chocolate smearing his fingers. 'Nothing about you is ridiculous, Liana.'

'I know I haven't experienced much of life.'

'And why is that?'

She paused, pressed her lips together. 'I don't know.'

But he thought she did. She must at least have a good guess. No need to press her now, though. Instead he held out the strawberry once more. 'Try it.'

She hesitated, her lips still pursed, everything in her resisting. Then he saw the moment when she made the decision to be different, and with a little shrug and a smile she reached for it. He drew back, his eyes glinting challenge. 'Open your mouth.'

Her eyes widened and for a second he thought he'd pushed too far. Too hard. But she did as he said, parting her lips so he could hold the strawberry out to her. He felt his groin harden and ache as she touched the tip of her pink tongue to the chocolate and licked.

'Mmm.' She sounded so sweetly innocent and yet as seductive as a siren as she gazed at him with eyes as wide and clear as lakes. He could drown in them. He was drowning, lost in this moment as she licked the chocolate again. 'I don't think I knew what I've been missing,' she said huskily, and he knew she wasn't just talking about a single, simple strawberry.

'Liana…' His voice was a groan as she bit into the strawberry, juice trickling down her chin, chocolate smearing her lush lips.

She ate it in two bites, and then Sandro could hold back no longer. He reached for her, dragging his hands through her hair as he brought her face to his and kissed her strawberry-sweet lips.

She tasted better, sweeter than any strawberry. And he wanted her more than he'd wanted anything or anyone before in his life. He kissed her deeply, as if he was drawing the essence of her right out of her mouth and into himself. Wanting and needing to feel her closer than a kiss, with his hands spanning her waist he drew her onto his lap, fitted her legs around him so she pressed snugly against his arousal and he flexed his hips against hers, craving that exquisite friction.

'Now, that's better,' he murmured and she let out a choked laugh.

'Sandro—' She broke off, her head buried in his neck, and Sandro stilled.

He was moving too fast. He'd forgotten, in the sweet spell of that kiss, that she was a virgin. Untouched. Inexperienced.

Sandro closed his eyes and willed the tide of his desire

back. Even so it misted his mind with a red haze. Gently he eased her off his lap.

'Sorry. Lost my head a bit there.'

'It's okay,' she murmured, but her face was still buried in his neck.

Sandro leaned back against the sofa cushions and tried, without success, to will away the ache in his groin.

'Sex doesn't scare me, you know,' she said suddenly, and he suppressed a smile.

'I'm very glad to hear it.'

'It's just…' She licked her lips, sending a shaft of lust burrowing deep into him. *Painful*. 'Everything else does. About…being with someone.'

'What do you mean?'

'Intimacy. Like you said. Sharing things. Being— vulnerable.'

He smiled, tried to draw her into that smile, into something shared. 'None of it is a walk in the park, is it?'

'You mean it scares you too?'

'Sometimes.' He was the one to glance away now. 'I'm not exactly an expert in all this myself, you know, Liana.'

'But you've had loads of relationships, according to the media anyway.'

'Don't believe everything you read.'

Her eyebrows rose, two pale arcs. 'It's not true?'

He shifted in his seat, uncomfortable to impart so much, yet knowing he could only be honest with this woman. His wife. 'I've had quite a few…sexual relationships, I admit. They didn't mean anything to me.'

'That's more than I've had,' she said with a soft laugh that wobbled at the end, a telling note.

He felt a sudden stab of surprising regret for all the pointless encounters he'd had, all attempts to stave off the loneliness and need he'd felt deep inside. The need that was, amazingly, starting to be met by this woman.

'Have you ever…loved anyone?' Liana asked softly. 'I mean, a woman? A romantic… Well, you know.'

'Yes.' Sandro paused, pictured Teresa. What had drawn him to her originally? She'd been so different from everything about his former life, he supposed. A California girl, with sun-kissed hair and bright blue eyes, always ready to laugh, always up for a good time. It had taken him nearly a year to realise Teresa only wanted a good time. With his money. His status. She wasn't interested in the man he really was, didn't want to do the whole 'for better or for worse' thing. At least, not for worse.

'Sandro?' Liana's soft voice interrupted the bleakness of his thoughts. 'You must have loved her very much.'

'Why do you say that?'

'Because your face is like a thundercloud.'

He shook his head. 'I thought I loved her.'

'Is there really a difference?'

He sighed. 'Maybe not. Sometimes disillusionment is worse than heartbreak.'

'How were you disillusioned?'

He shrugged, half amazed he was telling her all of this. 'I thought she loved me for me. But I discovered she was really only interested in my money and status, and not so much me, or being faithful to me.' He'd caught her in bed with the landscaping guy, of all people. She hadn't even been sorry.

Liana pressed her lips together. 'So that's why you're so suspicious.'

'Suspicious?'

'Of me.'

He hesitated then, because as much as he'd been enjoying their conversation and this new, startling intimacy, her words reminded him that she had agreed to marry him for exactly those reasons. Money. Power. A title.

Nothing had really changed, except maybe in his own sentimental mind.

He pushed the thought away; he wanted, for once, to enjoy the simple pleasure of being with a woman. With his wife. 'Have another strawberry,' he said, and held another one out to her parted lips.

Liana licked the last of the chocolate from her lips, every sense on impossible overload. She'd never felt so much— the sweetness of the strawberry, the seductive promise of his kiss, the alarming honesty of their conversation that left her feeling bare and yet bizarrely, beautifully light, as if she'd slipped the first tiny bit of a burden she'd been carrying so long she'd forgotten it was weighing her down. Crippling her.

This was why people fell in love, she supposed. This was what the magazines and romance novels hinted at— and yet she didn't even love Sandro. How could she, when she barely knew him?

And yet he was her husband, and he'd held her all night long and kissed her as if he couldn't get enough. She'd had more with him already than she'd ever had before, and if that made her pathetic, fine. She was pathetic. But for the first time in her life she could almost glimpse happiness.

But could he? Could they have something other than a marriage of convenience, even if they wanted it? Her own emotions and desires were a confused tangle, and she had no idea what Sandro's were. What he thought. What he felt. She didn't want to ask.

'What are you thinking about?' Sandro asked as he popped a strawberry into his own mouth.

'Lots of things.'

'You're all sunlight and shadows, smiling one minute, frowning the next.'

'Am I?' She laughed a little, tried for some more of this hard honesty. 'I guess I'm trying to figure out what I think. What I feel.'

'Maybe,' Sandro suggested softly, 'you should stop thinking so much. Just run with it.'

She nodded. Yes, that seemed like a good idea. Stop analysing. Stop worrying. Just…feel.

She'd spent half a lifetime trying not to feel, and now that was all she wanted to do. She laughed aloud, the sound soft and trembling, and Sandro smiled.

'Good idea?' he asked and she nodded again.

'Yes,' she answered with a smile. 'Good idea.'

They arrived in Los Angeles tired and jet-lagged, but Liana was still euphoric. This was a new place, a new day. A new life.

A limo was waiting for them at the airport, and Liana kept her nose nearly pressed on the glass as they drove through the city to Sandro's beachside villa in Santa Monica.

'I've never been to the US before, you know,' she said as she took in the impressive elegance of Rodeo Drive, the iconic Hollywood sign high above them.

'Consider yourself a tourist. I have some work to do, but we can do the sights.'

'What are the sights?'

'The usual museums and theme parks. The beach. I'd like to take you to a spa resort out in Palm Desert and pamper you to death.'

She let out a little laugh as a thrill ran through her. 'That sounds like a pretty good way to go.'

'I don't think you've ever been pampered,' Sandro said quietly. 'Spoiled.'

'Who would want to be spoiled?'

'I mean…' He shrugged, spread his hands. 'Treated. Indulged. Given an experience just to enjoy and savour.'

No, she'd never had any of those things, not remotely. 'Well, good thing I'm with you, then,' she said lightly. 'Pamper away.'

Sandro smiled and let it drop; she knew he knew there were things she wasn't saying, things she was afraid to say. And would she ever tell him? She thought of his fingers stroking her back, her hip, softening her. *Slowly, slowly.*

The limo pulled up to Sandro's gated mansion and they spent the next hour walking through it. He showed her the voice-controlled plasma-screen television, the shower stall big enough for two people that was activated by simply placing your palm on the wall.

'This place is like something out of James Bond,' she said with a laugh. 'I had no idea you were a gadget guy.'

'I worked in IT.'

'And Leo does too, doesn't he? I remember someone saying at our reception that he's drafting an IT bill.'

'He is.' Sandro's expression seemed to still, everything in him turn wary. 'He's worked hard in my absence.'

She heard the note of recrimination in his voice that she'd sensed before and she wanted to ask him about it. Wanted to know if he struggled with guilt the way she did. But the sun was so bright and they'd been having so much fun exploring his house that she didn't want to weigh down the lightness of the moment.

And, she knew, she was a coward.

They had lunch out on the private beach in front of the house, although Liana's body clock was insisting it

was some impossible, other time. She stretched her legs
out on the sun-warmed sand and gazed out at the Pacific,
started to fall halfway asleep.

Or maybe it was all the way asleep, because she startled to wakefulness when Sandro scooped her up in his
arms.

'Time for bed, I think,' he murmured, and carried her
across the sand and into the house. She sank onto the silk
sheets of his king-size bed and felt the mattress dip as
Sandro lay next to her, his arm still around her.

He drew her against him so her head rested on his
shoulder, the steady thud of his heart under her cheek.
Liana let out a little breathy sigh of contentment. How
had she gone without this all of her life?

She must have fallen asleep, because she awoke in
the middle of the night, the room drenched in darkness
save for a sliver of moonlight that bisected the floor. The
space in the bed next to her yawned emptily.

Liana shook her hair out of her face and glanced
around the bedroom, but Sandro was nowhere to be seen.
On bare feet she padded through the upstairs looking for
him, wondering where he'd gone—and why he'd left her
in the middle of the night.

She finally found him downstairs in his study, dressed
only in a pair of black silk pyjama bottoms, just as he had
been on their wedding night. He had his laptop in front
of him and papers were scattered across his desk. He
worked so hard, she thought with a twist of guilty regret.
She'd accused him of neglecting his royal duty, of being
someone she couldn't respect, but she was beginning to
see just how far from the truth that accusation had been.

'Can't sleep?' she asked softly and he glanced up, the
frown that had settled between his brows smoothed away
for a moment.

'My body clock is completely out of sync. I thought I might as well get some work done.'

'What are you working on?'

'Just tying up some loose ends with DT.'

'DT?'

'Diomedi Technology.'

She came into the room, driven by a new and deeper curiosity to know this man. To understand him. 'You founded it, didn't you? When you…moved?'

The smile he gave her was twisted, a little bitter. 'You mean when I abandoned my royal duty to pursue my own pleasures?'

She winced. 'Don't, Sandro.'

'It's true, though.'

'I'm not sure it is.'

'And how do you figure that, Liana?' His voice held a hard edge but she had a feeling for once it wasn't for her. He was angry with himself for leaving, for somehow failing. She knew because she understood that feeling too well. The churning guilt and regret for doing the wrong thing or, in her case, nothing at all.

Briefly she closed her eyes, willed the memory of Chiara's desperate gaze away, at least for this moment. Her sister's face, she knew, would haunt her for the rest of her life.

'I think there's always more to the story than there first appears,' she said quietly, coming to perch on the edge of his desk. 'You told me leaving felt necessary at the time, but you didn't tell me why.'

He glanced down at the papers on his desk. 'I didn't think we had that sort of relationship.'

Her breath hitched and she willed it to even out again. 'We didn't. But—but maybe we do now. Or at least, we're trying to.'

He glanced up at her then, everything about him inscrutable. Fathomless. 'Are we?'

Liana stared back at him, words on her lips and fear in her heart. This was the moment when she should show her hand, she knew. Her heart. Tell him that in the few days since they'd been married she'd started to change. He'd changed her, and now she wanted things she'd never let herself want. Affection. Friendship. *Love.*

The words were there and they trembled on her lips but then the fear of exposing so much want and need made her swallow them and offer a rather watery smile instead.

'You tell me.'

Wrong answer, she knew. A coward's answer. Sandro looked away. 'I don't know, Liana. I don't know what secrets you're hiding, or why you've, as you said yourself, experienced so little of life. It's almost as if you've kept yourself from it, from enjoying or feeling anything, and I won't know why or understand you until you tell me.' He glanced back at her then, his expression settled into resolute lines. 'But I'm not even sure you really want that. You told me you married me because of the opportunities being queen would give this charity of yours. Has that changed?'

She swallowed. 'No, not exactly.' Sandro's expression tightened and he started shuffling his papers into piles. 'But I've changed, Sandro, at least a little. I want to get to know you. And I hope you want to know me.' And that, Liana thought with a weary wryness, was about as honest as she could make herself be right now.

Sandro gazed at her thoughtfully. 'And how do you propose we do that?'

'Get to know one another, you mean?' She licked her lips, saw Sandro's gaze drop to her mouth, and felt warmth curling low in her belly. 'Well…as we have been doing. Talking. Spending time with one another.'

'We can talk all you like, but until you tell me whatever it is you're keeping from me, I don't think much is going to change.'

'But I told you I've already changed,' she said quietly. 'A little, at least. You've changed me.'

'Have I?' Sandro asked softly. He was still staring at her mouth and Liana felt a heavy languor begin to steal through her veins, making her feel almost drunk, reckless in a way she so rarely was. 'I can think of another way we could get to know one another,' she whispered.

He arched an eyebrow, heat flaring in his eyes, turning them to molten silver. 'And what would that be?'

'This.' She leaned forward, her heart thudding hard, and brushed her lips across his.

His mouth was cool and soft, his lips only barely parted, and he didn't respond as she'd expected him to, pulling her in his arms and taking control. No, he was waiting to see what she would do. How far she would go.

Emboldened, Liana touched her tongue to the corner of Sandro's mouth, heard his groan, felt it in the soft rush of breath against her own lips. Desire bit deeper, and she brought her hands up to his shoulders, steadying herself on the edge of his desk as she kissed him again, slid her tongue into his mouth with a surge of pure sexual excitement she thrilled to feel.

'Liana…' Sandro's hands tangled in her hair as he fastened his mouth more securely on hers, taking the kiss from her and making it his. Theirs.

And what a kiss it was. Liana could easily count the number of times she'd been kissed, half of them by Sandro, but this kiss was something else entirely. This kiss was shared, a giving and a taking and most of all an admission. A spilling of secrets, a confession of desire.

It felt like the most honest thing she'd ever done.

And then it was more than a kiss as Sandro swept all his papers aside and hauled her across the desk. She came willingly, sliding onto his lap, her legs on either side of him as she felt the hard, insistent press of his arousal against her and pleasure spiked deep inside.

Sandro deepened the kiss, his hands moving over her, cupping her breasts, the thin cotton of her sundress already too much between them. In that moment she wasn't afraid of her own feelings, the strength of her own desire—and his. She just wanted more.

Recklessly Liana pulled the dress over her head and tossed it to the floor. Sandro's gaze darkened with heat and then she unclasped her bra and sent it flying too. She was wearing only her panties, and even that felt like too much clothing.

'You're so beautiful,' he whispered huskily as his hands roved over her. 'Your skin is like marble.'

A small smile twitched her lips. 'Like a statue?'

He glanced up at her, his hands now cupping her breasts, his thumbs brushing over their taut peaks. 'Like Venus de Milo.' And then he put his mouth to her breasts and if she were a statue she came alive under him, writhing and gasping as he teased her with his tongue and lips.

She tangled her hands in his hair, arching her back and pressing against him, gasping aloud when he flexed his hips upwards and she felt the promise of what was to come, of what it would feel like to have him inside her, to be part of him. She wanted it now.

Sandro let out a shaky groan. 'Not here, Liana. Let me take you to bed—'

'Why do we need a bed?' she murmured and she slid

his hands up his bare chest, fingers spreading across hot skin and hard muscle.

'Your first time—'

'Are there rules about a woman's first time? Does it have to be on a bed, with roses and violins?'

He let out a shaky laugh. 'I don't have any roses at the moment—'

'I don't actually like roses.' She pressed against him, muscles she hadn't known she had tightening, quivering. 'Or violins.'

'Even so—'

'I want this.' She might not be able to be honest about everything yet, but she could be honest about this. About this real, rushing desire she felt. 'I want you. And I want you here, now, just like this.'

He eased away from her, but only to hold her face in his palms and search her expression. She stared back, firm in her purpose, clear-headed even in the midst of the haze of sexual desire. 'You want me,' he said slowly, almost wonderingly, and she leaned forward so her breasts brushed his chest and her lips touched his.

'I want you,' she whispered against his mouth, and then she kissed him again, another honest kiss, deeper this time, drawing everything from him even as she gave it back.

She'd never grow tired of this, she thought hazily as Sandro kissed his way down her body and her head fell back. She'd never have enough of this, of him. Her breath came out in short gasps as his fingers skimmed the waistband of her panties and then with one swift tug tore the thin cotton and tossed them aside, along with his own pyjama bottoms.

The sudden feel of his fingers against her most sensitive flesh made her let out a surprised cry, and all her muscles clenched as Sandro slid his fingers inside her.

She dropped her head on his shoulder, her fingernails biting into his back as he moved his hand with such delicious certainty and a wave of pleasure so intense and fierce it almost hurt crashed over her.

'Sandro.' Her breath came out in a shudder. 'Why didn't I know about this?'

'Because you didn't let yourself,' he murmured, and as his hand kept moving her hips moved of their own accord, her body falling into a rhythm as natural as breathing.

'I—I want you,' she gasped, each word coming out on a pant. 'I want you inside me.'

'It could hurt a little, your first—'

'Shut up about my first time,' she cut him off on a gasp, angling her hips so she was poised over him. She met his hot gaze as she sank slowly onto him, her eyes widening as she felt herself open and stretch. Her hands gripped his shoulders, and his hands were fastened to her hips, their bodies joined in every way. 'Nothing about this hurts.'

That wasn't quite true. Nothing hurt, but the feel of him inside her was certainly eye-opening. *Intense.* And wonderful. Intimate in a way she'd always been afraid to be. To feel.

She never wanted to go back to numbness again.

Sandro's gaze stayed on hers as he began to move, his hands on her hips guiding her to match his rhythm.

'Okay?' he murmured and she laughed, throwing her head back as pleasure began shooting sparks deep inside her, jolts of sensation that made speech almost impossible.

'More than okay,' she answered when she trusted her voice. 'Wonderful.'

And then words failed her as sensation took over, and Sandro's body moved so deeply inside hers she felt as if he touched her soul.

Maybe he did, because when the feelings finally took over, swamping her completely so her voice split the still air with one jagged cry of pleasure, she knew she'd never felt as close to a human being before, or ever.

And it felt more than wonderful. It felt as if he'd brought her back to life.

CHAPTER EIGHT

THEY HAD FIVE days in California, five days of seeing the sights and enjoying each other's company and each other's bodies. Making love.

That was what it felt like to Sandro, what it *was*. He was falling in love with his wife, with the warm woman who had broken through the coldness and the ice.

Looking at her as they strolled down the pier in Santa Monica, Sandro could hardly believe Liana was the same coolly composed woman he'd met two months ago. She wore a sundress in daffodil yellow, her pale hair streaming about her shoulders, her eyes sparkling and her cheeks flushed. She looked incandescent.

Her step slowed as she glanced at him, her brow wrinkling. 'You're giving me a funny look.'

'Am I?'

'Do I have ice cream on my face or something?' She'd been eating a chocolate ice cream with the relish usually exhibited by a small child, and every long lick had desire arrowing inside him and making him long to drag her back to his house and make love to her in yet another room. So far they'd christened his study, his bedroom, the shower, the beach, and the front hall when they'd been in too much of a rush to get any farther inside. At this rate, Santa Monica pier would be next, and damn the crowds.

'I'm just enjoying watching you eat your ice cream.'

'Is it really that fascinating?' She laughed and Sandro felt himself go hard as she took another lick, her pink tongue swiping at the chocolate with a beguiling innocence.

'Trust me, it is.'

She faltered midlick as she took in the hotness of his gaze, and then with an impish little smile she leaned forward and gave him a chocolatey kiss. 'That's to tide you over till later.'

'How much later?'

'I want to walk to the end of the pier.'

Sandro groaned and took her arm. 'You're going to kill me, woman.'

'You'll die with a smile on your face, though.'

'Or else a grimace of agony because you're too busy enjoying your ice cream to satisfy your husband.'

She arched her eyebrows in mock innocence. 'I believe I satisfied my husband twice today already, and it's not even noon. I think you might need to talk to a doctor.'

'I might,' he agreed. 'Or maybe you just need to stop eating ice cream in front of me.' And then because he couldn't keep himself from it any longer, he pulled her towards him and kissed her again, deeper this time, more than just something to tide him over until he could get her alone.

The ice-cream cone dangled from Liana's fingers and then fell to the pier with a splat as she kissed him back, looping her arms around his neck to draw his body against her pliant softness, and he very nearly lost his head as everything in him ached to finish what they'd started right there, amidst the rollerbladers and sunworshippers.

And Liana must have agreed with him, because she

kept kissing him, with all the enthusiasm he could ever want from a woman.

A woman he was falling in love with, and damn if he didn't want to stop.

A flashbulb going off made him ease back. The paparazzi hadn't bothered them too much since they'd arrived in LA; there were enough famous people in this town to make Sandro, thankfully, just another celebrity. But having his hands all over his wife in public was front-page fodder for sure.

'Sorry,' he said, and eased back. 'That's going to be in the papers, I'm afraid.'

'I don't care,' Liana answered blithely. 'We're married, after all.' She glanced down at their feet. 'But you'd better buy me another ice cream.'

'Not a chance.' Sandro tugged her by the hand back down the pier. 'I won't be answerable for my actions if I do.'

Several hours later they were lying in his bed—they'd made it there eventually, after christening another room of his beach house, this time the kitchen—legs and hands entwined, the mellow afternoon sunlight slanting over them.

And as much as Sandro never wanted any of it to end, he knew it had to.

'I've finished up with DT,' he said, sliding a hand along the smooth tautness of Liana's belly. 'We should return to Maldinia tomorrow.'

'Tomorrow?' He heard the dismay in her voice and then she sighed in acceptance, putting her hand over his and lacing her fingers through his. 'It went by so fast. I don't think I've ever enjoyed myself so much.'

'Me neither. But duty calls.' He heard the slightly sardonic note enter his voice, as it always did when he talked about his royal life, and he knew Liana heard it too.

She twisted towards him, her expression intent and earnest, her bare breasts brushing his chest. An interesting combination, and one that made Sandro want to kiss her again. And more.

'Why do you hate being king?' she asked, and he felt as if she'd just touched him with a branding iron. Pain, white-hot, lanced through him. Desire fled.

'Why do you think I hate being king?' he answered, glad his voice stayed even.

'Maybe hate is too strong a word. But whenever you talk about it—about Maldinia and the monarchy—you get this…*tone* to your voice. As if you can't stand it.'

He started to shift away from her, sliding his fingers from her own, but she tugged him back, or at least stayed him for a moment. 'Don't, Sandro,' she said quietly. 'I'm not trying to offend you or make you angry. I just want to know you.'

'I think you've known me pretty well this week, wouldn't you say?'

Her expression clouded, her eyes the colour of bruises. 'But that's just sex.'

'Just sex? I'm offended.'

'All right, fine. Amazing sex, but still, I want to know more than your body, as fantastic as that is.'

He stared at her then, saw the shadows in her eyes, the uncertain curve of her mouth. 'Do you really, Liana?' he asked quietly. 'We've had a wonderful time this past week, I'll be the first to admit it. But we haven't talked about anything really personal and I think you've liked it that way.'

Her lips trembled before she firmed them into a line and nodded. 'Maybe I do. I'm a private person, Sandro, I admit that. There are—things I don't like talking about. But I still want to get to know you. Understand you.'

'So I bare my soul while you get to keep yours hidden? Doesn't sound like much of a fair trade to me.'

'No, it doesn't.' She was silent for a moment, nibbling her lip, clearly wrestling with herself. Sandro just waited. He had no idea what she was going to say or suggest, and he felt a wariness leap to life inside him because he might accuse her of keeping things back, but he knew he was too.

About his family. His father. Himself.

'How about this,' she finally said, and she managed to sound both resolute and wavering at the same time. It made Sandro want to gather her up in his arms and kiss her worries away, as well as his own. That would be far more enjoyable than talking. 'We ask each other questions.'

He frowned, still wary. 'Questions?'

'Sounds simple, doesn't it?' she agreed with a wry smile that tugged at his heart. And other places. 'What I mean is we take turns. You ask me a question and I have to answer it. Then I get to ask you a question and you have to answer it.' She eyed him mischievously, although he could still tell this was big for her. And for him. Honesty, intimacy? He might crave it but that didn't make it easy. 'I'll even,' she added, 'let you go first.'

Sandro took a deep breath, let it out slowly. He nodded. 'Okay.'

'Okay. Ask me the first question.' Liana scrambled into a seated position, her legs crossed, her expression alert. She was completely naked and Sandro didn't know whether he wanted to ask her a question or haul her into his arms. No, actually he did.

Sex would be easier. Safer. And far more pleasurable.

But he'd accused Liana of holding things back and he'd be both a coward and a hypocrite now if he was the one to pull away. He drew another deep breath and sifted through all the things he'd wondered about his wife. 'Why have you devoted your life to Hands To Help?'

She inhaled sharply, just once, and then let it out slowly. 'Because my sister had epilepsy.'

Surprise flashed through him. 'You've never mentioned—'

She held up one slender palm. 'Nope, sorry. My turn now.'

'Okay.' He braced himself for the question he knew she would ask, the question she'd asked before. *Why do you hate being king?* And how would he answer that? Nothing about that answer was simple. Nothing about it was something he wanted to say.

'Why did you choose California?' she asked, and his jaw nearly dropped. She was gazing at him steadily and he knew with a sudden certainty that she was going easy on him. Because she knew how hard he'd found her first question. And yet he'd cut right to the quick with his own. He felt a surge of feeling for this woman who had shown him in so many ways just how strong and deep and wonderful she was.

'I chose California because I wanted to go into IT and it was a good place for start-up businesses. Also, for the weather.'

She smiled, just slightly, and he felt herself tense for his next question. 'What's your sister's name?' he asked, and to his surprise and recrimination her eyes filled with tears. He'd meant it to be an easy question, but obviously it wasn't.

'Chiara.' She drew a clogged breath. 'I called her Chi-Chi.'

The past tense jumped out at him and he realised what

a moron he was. He should have realised her sister was no longer alive. 'What—?'

She shook her head. 'My turn.' She blinked rapidly until the tears receded, although Sandro would have rather they'd fallen. When, he wondered, had Liana last cried? He had a feeling it had been a long, long time ago.

'What made you renounce your inheritance?'

It felt necessary at the time. That was what he'd told her before. He could say the same now, but it wasn't really much of an answer. He gazed at her steadily, saw the remnant of old sorrow in her eyes even as she gazed unblinkingly back. 'Because I thought I'd lose myself—my soul—if I stayed.'

'Why—?'

'Fair's fair. My turn now.'

'All right.'

He saw her brace herself, everything in her tensing for his next question. 'How did your sister die?' he asked softly.

For a second, no more, her features twisted in a torment that made him want to lean forward to embrace her, comfort her, but then her expression blanked again and she said quietly, 'She choked during an epileptic fit when she was four years old.'

This time he didn't keep himself from reaching for her. 'God, Liana. I'm sorry.' No wonder she devoted herself to her damned charity, to supporting the families of children like Chiara. She remained in his arms, stiff and unyielding as he stroked her hair, her shoulder. 'How old were you when it happened?'

'Eight.' She drew a shuddering breath. 'But that's two questions from you, so I get two now.'

'We could stop—'

'Not a chance.' She eased back, dabbed at her eyes with one hand before she stiffened her shoulders, gave him a look of stony determination.

'Why did you feel as if you'd lose yourself, your soul, if you stayed in Maldinia?'

They were drawing the big guns now, Sandro thought wryly. Asking and admitting things that made them both very uncomfortable. Terribly vulnerable. 'Because I couldn't stand all the hypocrisy.'

'What hypocrisy?'

'It's my turn now—'

'No.' She shook her head, her pale hair flying over her shoulders. 'I get two questions in a row, remember.'

'Damn.' He smiled wryly, sighed. 'The hypocrisy of my parents as well as myself.'

'What—?'

'Nope.' He shook his head now. 'My turn.'

She closed her eyes, and he felt as if she was summoning strength. 'Go ahead.'

'What was your favourite subject in school?'

Her eyes flew open and she stared at him in surprise, before a small smile tugged at her mouth. 'Art. What was yours?'

'Computers.'

They stared at each other for a long moment, the only sound their breathing, the rustle of covers underneath their naked bodies. 'Do you want to stop?' Liana asked softly, and he realised he didn't. He wanted to tell everything to this woman, bare his soul and his heart along with his body. And he wanted her to do it too, and, more importantly, to want to. He wanted that intimacy. That vulnerability. That trust, that love.

And he hoped to God that Liana wanted it too.

* * *

Liana held her breath while Sandro's gaze roved over her and then he smiled and shook his head.

'No, let's keep going. My turn to ask now.'

She nodded, steeling herself. It was almost a relief to answer his questions, like lancing a wound or easing an intense pressure. But it also hurt, and while he might have given her a break with the last question she didn't think he would now.

'Why didn't you go to university?'

'Because I wanted to start working with Hands To Help as soon as I could.' That one, at least, was easy, even if it most likely made him think she was a bit obsessive about her charity. That was because he didn't know the whole truth about Chiara; he hadn't asked. And she wasn't, she acknowledged, going to admit it unless he did.

Now her turn. She eyed him, his body relaxed and so incredibly beautiful as he lay stretched out across from her, unashamedly naked, the late afternoon sunlight glinting off his burnished skin, the perfect tautness of his muscled body. 'How were your parents hypocrites?'

He didn't say anything for a long moment, his gaze drawn and thoughtful, and finally Liana prompted him softly. 'Sandro?'

'It's not just a one-sentence answer.'

'We didn't make a rule about answers having to only be one sentence.'

'But it's easier, isn't it?' He glanced up at her, eyes glinting even as his mouth twisted with something like bitterness. 'We're both revealing as little information as we can.'

She couldn't deny that. 'So we start small,' she said with a shrug. 'No one said this had to be a complete confessional.'

'My parents were hypocrites because they only pretended that they loved us when there was a camera or reporter around. When it mattered.'

'Why—?'

'Nope. My turn.' So he was sticking with a one-sentence answer. She gave a little shrug of assent and waited, wondering just what he would ask her next. 'What do you fantasise about doing with me that we haven't done already?'

Shock had her jaw dropping even as heat blazed through her at his heavy-lidded look. 'Umm…' Her mind was blank, spinning. 'Going to the cinema?'

He let out a low, throaty chuckle. 'I see I'm going to have to rephrase that question.'

Her cheeks warmed. She might have been unabashed with him in the bedroom—or whatever room it happened to be—but talking about it felt different. More revealing somehow. 'My turn,' she said, her voice nearly a croak as she willed her blush to fade. She was suddenly, achingly conscious that they were both naked. That they'd just made love but already she wanted to again. And so, it seemed, judging from his words as well as the proud evidence of his body, did Sandro.

'What's your question, Liana?' Sandro asked in a growl. 'Because the way you're looking at me, I'm not going to give you the time to ask me.'

'Sorry.' She jerked her gaze up to his face, tried to order her dazed thoughts. 'Umm… How were you a hypocrite?'

'Because I bought into their lies and when I realised that's what they were I kept it going.' He tossed the words away carelessly, but they made Liana want to ask more. Understand more.

'My turn now,' Sandro said, his voice a growl of sexual

intent. 'Now I'll rephrase my last question. What do you fantasise about doing with me *sexually* that we haven't already done?'

Just the question, in that husky murmur of his, made her breasts ache and her core throb. 'We've already done a lot….'

'Are you saying there isn't something?' Sandro asked silkily, his tone suggesting that he knew otherwise.

'No, not exactly….'

'Then what? Play by the rules, Liana. Answer the question.'

She pressed her hands to her face. 'This is embarrassing.'

'Why?'

'I—I don't know.'

'I think you do.'

'Fine, if you know so much, you tell me what I fantasise about.'

He laughed softly. 'I don't think so. You're not going to get off that easily.' His mouth curved in a wicked smile. 'No pun intended. But I will tell you what I fantasise about.'

'Okay,' she breathed, and Sandro leaned forward, all predatory power and sexual intent.

'I fantasise about tasting you.' Liana inhaled sharply and felt her insides turn liquid. 'And I don't mean your mouth.'

She let out a wobbly laugh. 'I might be inexperienced, but I didn't think that's what you meant.'

'I want to taste you, Liana. I want to feel you tremble against me while I do.'

She closed her eyes, images, amazing, explicit images, blitzing through her brain, making it impossible to think. To respond. And yet the words came of themselves and with her eyes still closed she heard herself whisper, 'I want that too.'

And then Sandro was reaching for her and kissing her, his mouth hard and hot and yet so very sweet. His hands slid down her body as his tongue delved deep and Liana tangled her fingers in his hair, drawing him closer, needing him more.

But then he began to move his mouth down her body and she knew where he was going, knew what he wanted—and what she wanted. Everything in her seemed to still and hang suspended, waiting, yearning—

And then her breath came out in a sudden gasp of pleasure as he spread her thighs and put his mouth to her, his tongue flicking against the sensitive folds, everything in her exposed and open and vulnerable.

It was exquisite. Unbearable. *Too much.* Too much pleasure, too much openness, too much feeling. She felt his breath against her heated, tender skin and she let out a choked gasp, felt tears start in her eyes. Tears that felt like the overflow of emotion in her soul.

'*Sandro...*'

He lifted his head slightly. 'Do you want me to stop?'

'*No—*'

And then he tasted her again, deeper still, his mouth moving over her so surely, and her thighs clenched, her hands fisting in his hair as she cried out her climax and tears trickled down her cheeks. She felt as if she'd been broken and put together again; as if Sandro had reconstructed her.

He rested his cheek against her tummy as her heart rate slowed and she wiped the tears from her face with trembling fingers.

Gently he reached up and took her hands from her face, wiping the remaining tears away with his thumbs.

'I'm sorry,' she whispered.

'Sorry? What on earth for?'

'For crying—'

'I don't mind your tears, Liana.' He kissed her navel. 'You're amazing,' he said softly and she let out a shaky laugh.

'I feel as weak as a kitten.'

'Amazing,' he repeated, and Liana had a sudden, over-whelming urge to tell him she loved him, but she kept the words back. Despite what they'd just done, it felt like too much too soon.

So instead she decided to admit to her fantasy and pay him in kind.

Gently she pushed at his shoulder and he lifted his head, his chin resting on her tummy, to gaze at her, his expression sleepy and hooded. 'It's your turn now,' she said, and that sleepy gaze became suddenly alert.

'My turn?'

She pushed him again and with a smile he rolled over onto his back, everything about him masculine, magnificent, *hers*. 'Fair's fair,' she said and, with a blaze of sensual anticipation and ancient, feminine power, she straddled his thighs, bent her head so her mouth brushed his navel—and then moved lower.

CHAPTER NINE

LIANA GAZED AT her reflection and tried to still the nervous fluttering in her stomach. They'd been back in Maldinia for a week, and tonight was the fundraiser for Hands To Help.

In the week since they'd returned from California, they'd continued exploring the sexual side of their relationship with joyous abandon. The nights were pleasure-filled, and the days…?

Liana wasn't so sure about the days. They'd both been busy with royal duties, but there had still been time to spend just with each other—if they had wanted to. Sandro, however, hadn't sought her out. They certainly hadn't had any more question-and-answer sessions, and the most honest either of them seemed to be was with their bodies. Not their words. Not their hearts.

It was ironic, really, that she wanted that now. She'd entered this marriage because she'd believed it would be convenient, that it *wouldn't* involve her heart. She hadn't wanted love or intimacy or any of it—and now she did.

Now she did so much, and Sandro was the one pulling away. She'd felt his emotional withdrawal from the moment they'd stepped off the royal jet. At first she'd thought he was just preoccupied with work; he'd spent the entire fourteen-hour flight from LA working in his study on the plane. But after a week of incredible sex and virtually no conversation, she knew work couldn't be the only reason.

She'd gone over what Sandro had told her about himself many times, yet those few terse sentences hardly gave anything away.

My parents were hypocrites because they only pretended that they loved us when there was a camera or reporter around. When it mattered.

Because I bought into their lies and when I realised that's what they were I kept it going.

What did it mean, he kept it going? And what, really, did his parents' lack of love have to do with being king? Unless he simply found the whole atmosphere of the palace too toxic to endure. Liana had to admit she always felt herself tense when the queen dowager was around. But to walk away from everything he'd known and been for fifteen whole years? There had to be more to his story, just as there was more to hers.

And even if she wanted to admit more to Sandro, he didn't seem willing or interested to hear it. He'd been perfectly polite, of course, even friendly, and at night he made her body sing. But they'd been teetering on the edge of a far deeper intimacy and since returning here Sandro had taken a few definite, determined steps back.

Which shouldn't, Liana told herself, make her feel restless. Anxious. Why couldn't she accept what they had and deem it enough? It was more than she'd ever had before, more than she'd ever let herself want.

And yet it wasn't enough. Not when she'd had a glimpse—a taste—of just how much more they could have.

Taking a deep breath, she forced her thoughts away from such pointless musings and inspected her reflection once more. She wore an emerald-green evening gown, a bold choice for her, and she'd selected it with the help of Demi, her stylist. She wondered what Sandro would think of the asymmetrical cut, with one shoulder left bare. She worn her hair up, but loosely, unlike the more severe chignons she used to favour. To finish the outfit she'd chosen diamond chandelier earrings and a matching necklace that had belonged to her mother.

She took a deep breath and turned away from the mirror. The maid, Rosa, who had helped her dress, smiled encouragingly. 'You look lovely, Your Highness.'

'Thank you, Rosa.'

Rosa handed her a matching wrap of emerald satin and Liana draped it over one arm before leaving her suite of rooms. The dress whispered against her legs as she walked down the corridor, her heart thudding harder with every step that took her towards Sandro. What would he think of her gown? And what would he think of *her*? Tonight was such an important night for her, finally bringing more visibility to Hands To Help, and yet in this moment she cared more about what Sandro thought than anything else. She wanted that intimacy back again, that closeness that didn't come from sex—as amazing as that was—but from simply being with one another. Talking and laughing in a way they hadn't since returning from California.

Sandro was waiting at the bottom of the palace's sweeping staircase as Liana came down. He looked dark and dangerous and utterly devastating in black tie, his hair brushed back, his eyes glittering like shards of silver.

He stilled as she approached, his expression going utterly blank as his gaze swept her from head to toe, making Liana wonder just what he thought. It was the first time she'd worn a formal gown since their marriage.

'You look beautiful,' he said quietly, and pleasure flared through her at the obvious sincerity of those simple words. 'That colour suits you.'

'Thank you,' she murmured. 'You do amazing things to a tuxedo.'

His mouth quirked in a smile and his eyes lightened to the colour of a dawn mist as he took her arm. 'I'd like to do amazing things to you,' he whispered as he drew her down the last few steps.

'And I'd like you to do them,' she answered back. 'I have a few amazing things up my sleeve as well.'

Sandro grinned, and even as familiar heat flared inside her Liana knew it wasn't enough. Sex wasn't enough, never would be. But now was surely not the time for a heart-to-heart. Perhaps later tonight they would talk again. Learn each other again.

Sandro's grin faded and Liana stilled, wondering what had changed, when he addressed a member of the palace staff, who came hurrying forward.

'Your Highness?'

'Please bring the crown jewels to my study. The emerald parure, I think.'

'Very good, Your Highness.'

'The crown jewels?' Liana repeated, and touched the chandelier necklace around her throat. 'But—'

'What you're wearing is very lovely,' Sandro said as he led her towards his study, one hand warm and firm on the small of her back. 'But there is a piece from the royal collection that would suit you—and that dress—perfectly. Do you mind?'

'Mind?' She shook her head. 'No, of course not.'

'Here you are, Your Highness.' The footman brought in a mahogany case inlaid with ivory, and placed it on the desk before handing Sandro the keys.

'Thank you,' Sandro murmured, and the man left as he unlocked the case and lifted the lid. Liana gasped at the sight of the glittering jewels within, and Sandro turned to her with a glint in his eye. 'Lovely, aren't they?' he murmured. 'Supposedly once owned by Napoleon.'

'For Josephine?'

'His empress. And you are my queen.'

His queen. Liana thrilled to the words, to their implication. She was his, heart and soul, whether he knew it or not. Whether he wanted it or not. Yet in this moment she felt only happiness as he lifted the heavy necklace from its velvet bed, the diamond-encrusted emeralds catching the light and twinkling as if lit with a fire from within. 'May I?' Sandro asked softly, and wordlessly she nodded, holding her breath as she felt his fingers, warm and sure, on the back of her neck.

Goosebumps rose on her flesh as he unclasped her diamond necklace and slid it from her, his fingers brushing the tender skin of her neck, the hollow of her throat. Liana bit her lip to keep a shudder of pure longing from escaping her. He reduced her to want so effortlessly, and yet she felt his own response, the strength of his own need as his fingers rested against her throat, his breath hitching slightly as it fanned the nape of her neck. She eased back against him, leaning against his chest, and his hands came around her shoulders, cradling her. For a perfect moment she felt completely at peace, wonderfully loved. He brushed his lips against her neck and then he steadied her again, before putting the emerald-and-diamond necklace around her throat, the stones heavy against her skin and warm from his hands.

He clasped the necklace and then rested his hands on her shoulders again, his fingers curling around her, seeming to reach right inside. 'Liana...' he began, his voice an ache, a caress, and everything in her longed to know what he was thinking. Feeling. And what he was going to say.

But he didn't say anything, just slid his hands from her shoulders and reached for the other pieces of the parure: earrings, bracelet, and a tiara.

'I've never actually worn a tiara,' Liana said as he placed it on her loose updo. 'Does it look ridiculous? As if…as if I'm trying to be a princess?'

'You're not a princess,' Sandro reminded her. 'You are a queen.'

Liana touched the stones, wanting once again to tell him she loved him. Had he been about to tell her the same thing? She didn't know whether she dared to hope, and she didn't say anything, just put on the earrings and bracelet.

'Thank you,' she said, when she was wearing all of the jewels. 'They're amazing.'

'You're amazing. They look beautiful on you. A true queen.'

She met his eyes, smiling, only to have her smile wobble and then slip completely from her face as she saw the frown settle between Sandro's brows, the darkness steal into his eyes. He might call her a true queen, but she didn't know then whether he wanted to be her king.

Sandro watched Liana from across the crowded ballroom where the fundraiser for Hands To Help was being held; she was talking to several dignitaries, a flute of champagne in one slender hand, her body resplendent, like an emerald flame, in that amazing dress, the light from the crystal chandeliers catching the strands of gold and silver in her moon-coloured hair. She looked beautiful, captivating, and every inch the consummate queen.

Sandro saw several men cast her covert, admiring

glances, and he felt his insides clench with a potent mix of jealousy, desire, and love.

He loved her. He hadn't told her, hadn't even wanted to tell her, not just because he didn't know if she loved him, but because he didn't trust his own feelings. His own self.

Hadn't he been wrong before? And while their time in California had been sweet, and their nights together since then even sweeter, he still didn't know if it was real.

Well, sex was real. Real and raw and powerful. But love? Could he love her after so short a time? What had happened to the icy, reserved woman he'd first met? Had she really changed—and had he?

Restlessly, Sandro shifted and took a sip of champagne. Watching Liana now, he felt a new and unwelcome realisation sweep over him. Here she was in her element; she was queen. He saw the sparkle in her eyes as she talked about Hands To Help, the regal bearing of her beautiful body. This, he thought, made her come alive in a way he hadn't seen before, even when she'd been in his arms. This was why she'd agreed to marry him in the first place, what gave her her whole reason for being.

To be queen.

And while that shouldn't bother him, he knew it did. Because while Liana made a beautiful and perfect queen, he didn't feel like her match.

He didn't deserve to be king.

If I could have, I'd have left you to rot in California, or, better yet, in hell.

So many months after his father's death, his savage nearly last words still had the power to hurt him. To make him question himself, just as he had so many years before. His father hadn't called him back from California because he'd wanted a reconciliation, as Sandro had so naively believed.

No, his father had asked him because he was desperate. Because the media mess of Leo and Alyse's marriage had seemed irredeemable. Sandro was the second choice.

He hadn't realised any of that until his father had died, three weeks after he'd called him in California. The former king had known he was terminally ill, had wanted to get the succession sorted out before his death.

Had really wanted Leo.

Sandro's gaze moved from his wife to his brother, chatting with a group of IT businessmen, Alyse by his side. Would Leo make a better king than him?

Sandro was sure of it.

And yet from the moment he'd returned Leo hadn't offered a single word of protest. He'd stepped aside gracefully, had accepted his position as cabinet minister with a nod and a smile. Leo, Sandro had to assume, was relieved. And why shouldn't he be?

Neither of them had wanted to follow in their father's footsteps. Neither of them had wanted the awful burden of royal duty.

And yet here they were.

One of the footmen flanking the room rang a bell, and Sandro watched as the crowd fell silent and with a shyly assured smile Liana went to the front of the room. Sandro watched her, felt a surge of admiration and love, and yet washed over it all was desperation. Because she was too good for him. Because he didn't believe she could really love him, a man who had shirked his duty for so long. A man who was second best.

'Thank you all so much for coming,' Liana said, her voice clear and musical. Sandro felt as if he could listen to her for ever. And everyone else must have too because the room went utterly silent as she spoke about Hands To Help's mission and what it meant to her.

She didn't, Sandro realised with a flicker of surprise, talk about her sister.

But he could hear the passion in her voice, the utter sincerity, and he knew everyone else could too. And when she was done the room broke out into an applause that was not merely polite, but spontaneous and sincere.

Sandro's gut twisted. How could this amazing woman love him?

She moved through the crowd, chatting with various guests, but he saw her gaze rove restlessly over the clusters of people and knew she was looking for him.

He came forward, smiling as he took her by the hand. 'Well done. You spoke beautifully, Liana.'

Pink touched her cheeks and her eyes sparkled. How had he ever thought she was a statue? Or icy and cold? In this moment she looked real, warm, vibrant, and glorious. He almost told her he loved her right then.

Almost.

But he didn't, because along with his other sins he was a coward. He didn't want to hear the silence he feared would be the answer back…just as it had been before.

Liana felt Sandro's preoccupation as they left the fundraiser and headed for their suite in the private family wing of the palace. It was past midnight and all around them the palace was dark and hushed, only a few sleepy footmen on duty.

'I think it went well tonight, don't you?' Liana said as they turned down the corridor that housed their suite of rooms.

'Very well.' His lips curved in a smile but his voice was toneless, and she had no idea what he was thinking. Feeling.

'Thank you for organising it,' she said, hating that she felt awkward, even if just a little. 'It was very thoughtful.'

'It was the least I could do.'

Sandro opened the door to his bedroom, the bedroom they'd shared since returning from California even though Liana had her own adjoining room.

Uncertainly she stepped in behind him, because she couldn't decipher his mood at all and she was getting so very tired of wondering. Worrying.

'Sandro—'

Before she could say another word she was in his arms, her back pressed against the door as he kissed her with a raw, rough intensity she hadn't felt before. It was a kiss of passion but it felt like grief. Even so it ignited everything inside her and she kissed him back, matching him even though part of her cried out that whatever was wrong between them, it couldn't be solved by sex.

Maybe Sandro disagreed. Or maybe sex was all he wanted, for he slid his hands down her satin-clad legs before sliding the material up to her hips. Heat flared as he pressed his hand against her, the thin silk of her panties the only barrier between them.

She put her hands on either side of his face, tried to get him to look at her. 'Sandro, what is it?' she whispered even as an insistent, pleasurable ache had started between her thighs, urged on by the press of his hand. 'What's wrong?'

'Nothing's wrong,' he answered, his voice thick with desire. 'I just need you, Liana. I want you. Now.' He hoisted her leg up and wrapped it around his hip, and as he kissed her again Liana closed her eyes, let the sensation wash over her.

She wanted him too, and while she wanted his honesty

more, she understood he needed this. Needed her. And maybe that could be enough, at least for now.

He buried his head in the curve of his neck, a shudder racking his body as he moved against her. Liana put her arms around him, drawing him even closer, and then he was inside her, and it felt as deep and overwhelming and as wonderful as always.

She met him thrust for thrust, gasping out his name, her head thrown back against the door, and afterwards as their hearts raced against each other and the sweat cooled on their skin Sandro whispered against her throat.

'I love you.'

Everything in Liana stilled, and she felt a fragile happiness emerge from the tumult of her emotions like the first bloom of spring, tender and new.

She smoothed his hair away from his face and kissed his lips. 'I love you too.'

Neither of them spoke, and even as they remained in each other's arms Liana wondered why that confession of love—something she'd longed for—made her feel sadder than ever.

CHAPTER TEN

SANDRO STARED UNSEEINGLY down at the various letters he'd been given by his secretary to sign. The words blurred in front of him and wearily he rubbed his eyes. He'd been working in his study all day, reviewing fiscal plans and budget cuts in preparation for a meeting with his cabinet tomorrow.

He could see Leo's mark on everything he read, from the proposal to extend broadband to most of the country—something his brother felt passionately about, just as he did—to the necessary budget cuts in the palace. Leo clearly would rather go without a few luxuries than cut anything that affected his people.

He would have made a good king, Sandro thought, not for the first time. If the press hadn't uncovered the whole marriage masquerade debacle, his brother would have been a great king. And he *would* have been king, because Sandro would have stayed in California. He wouldn't have come back. Wouldn't have married Liana.

Wouldn't have had any of it.

Sighing, he rubbed his temples, felt the beginnings of a headache.

A quick knock sounded and then Leo opened the door, closing it behind him.

'I'm heading home, but I just wanted to make sure you didn't need me for anything?'

'No, I think I'm ready for tomorrow.' He tapped the papers in front of him. 'I can see you've done a lot of good work here, Leo.'

Leo shrugged. 'Just doing my job.'

Sandro nodded, even as he felt that tension and awful uncertainty ratchet up inside him. And it had been Leo's job, for fifteen years. A hell of a long time. 'You did it well.'

'Thank you,' Leo answered, and Sandro heard the repressive note in his brother's voice, felt a pang of sorrow. Once, they'd been close, two small boys banding together. Now he felt a distance yawn between them and he had no idea how to close it.

He stared down at the papers again, wished he knew the words to say, and had the courage to say.

'Sandro?' Leo asked for a moment. 'Is everything all right…between you and Liana?'

'Between me and Liana?' Sandro's voice came out sharp. 'Why do you ask?'

Leo shrugged. 'Because I know you married for convenience, and yet I've seen the way you look at each other. Something's going on.'

'We're married, Leo. Of course something is going on.'

'Do you love her?'

Sandro felt his throat go tight. 'That's between Liana and me, isn't it?'

'Sorry. I don't mean to be nosy.' Leo sighed. 'I just want you to be happy.'

'And since you've just fallen in love you want everyone else to as well.'

'Something like that, I suppose.'

'Don't worry about Liana and me, Leo. We're fine.'
Sandro spoke with a firmness he didn't really feel, because they weren't fine. Not exactly. Ever since returning to Maldinia, he'd felt the emotional distance yawn
between them. Physically things were amazing, exciting.
But emotionally? He might have been honest and vulnerable and all that in California, but here? Where the
memories mocked him? When the fear that he didn't deserve any of this, couldn't live up to it, suffocated him?

No, not so emotionally available now. Here. Even if,
in a moment of weakness, he'd told her he loved her.

'Okay,' Leo said after a moment. 'Well. Goodnight.'

'Goodnight.'

It was early evening and a purple twilight was settling over the palace and its gardens as Sandro left his
study a few minutes after Leo. He and Liana had a dinner
engagement that evening, something official and most
likely boring at the Italian embassy.

But before he got ready for it, he wanted to see Liana.
Talk to her…although he had no idea what he was going
to say.

He found her in the pretty, feminine little room she
used as her own study, going over her schedule with her
private secretary. Sandro watched them for a moment,
two heads bent together, smiling and chatting as they re-
viewed certain points.

Liana was in her element, and that was brought home
to him no more so than when she looked up and smiled
her welcome.

'I've just been going over my schedule—it looks like
a very busy week!'

'Does it?' The secretary, Christina, excused herself,
and Sandro closed the door, leaning against it. 'So what
are you doing?'

'Well…' Liana glanced down at the typewritten sheet. 'On Monday I'm visiting the paediatric ward of the hospital here in Averne. Tuesday is a lunch for primary caregivers of disabled and elderly. Wednesday I'm meeting with a primary school, and Thursday I'm officially opening a new playground in the city's public gardens.' She looked up, eyes sparkling. 'I know I'm not inventing a cure for cancer or anything, but I like feeling so useful.'

'Surely you felt useful before, when you worked for Hands To Help.'

'Yes, I did,' Liana answered after a moment. 'Of course I did. But sometimes…' She trailed off, and, intrigued, Sandro stepped closer.

'Sometimes?'

Liana gave a little shrug. 'Sometimes it hurt, working there. It reminded me of—of my sister.'

'Do you miss her?' he asked quietly and she blinked rapidly, needlessly straightening the papers in front of her.

'Every day.'

'It must be hard. I didn't think many people actually died from epilepsy.'

'They don't.'

'So Chiara was just one of the unlucky ones?'

And for some reason this remark made her stiffen as if she'd suddenly turned to wood. 'Yes,' she said, and her voice was toneless. 'She was unlucky.'

Sandro stared at her, saw how the happiness and excitement had drained from her, and felt guilt needle him. Damn it, he'd done that. He shouldn't have asked those questions, and yet he'd just been trying to get to know her all over again. Get closer.

Yet you keep your secrets to yourself.

'I'm sorry I've been a bit—distant lately,' he said abruptly, and Liana looked up, startled.

'At least you noticed.'

'And you have too, I assume?'

'Yes.' Her voice was soft, sad. 'I know we've been— Well, the nights have been—' She laughed a little, shook her head. 'You know what I mean.'

'I certainly do.'

'But we haven't talked, really. Not since California.'

Not since they'd sat across from each other on his bed, naked not just with their bodies but with their souls. He sighed. 'Returning to this palace always brings back some bad memories for me. It's hard to combat them.'

'What memories, Sandro?'

He dragged his hand across his eyes as words burned in his chest, caught in his throat. How much to admit? To confess? 'A lot of memories.' She just waited, and he dropped his hand. 'Memories of my father always telling me how he was counting on me,' he said, his voice expressionless now. 'Counting on me to be a good king. Just like him.'

'Just like him?' Liana repeated softly, a slight frown curving her mouth downwards. She knew, just as the whole world did, that his father hadn't been a good king at all. He'd been dissolute, uninterested in his people, a spendthrift, a scoundrel, an arrogant and adulterous *ass*.

And Sandro had idolised him.

'He was my hero, growing up,' he said, and then laughed. 'Which sounds ridiculous, because you know as well as I do there was nothing heroic about him.'

'But you were a child.'

'I believed that until I was eighteen.' He winced just saying it aloud. 'I insisted on believing it, even when boys at boarding school taunted me with the truth, even when

I saw the newspaper headlines blaring about his affairs, his reckless spending.' He shook his head. 'I convinced myself they were jealous or just stirring up trouble. I insisted on believing he was a good man, even when everything showed me otherwise.'

'That's not something to be ashamed of, Sandro,' Liana said quietly. 'Believing the best of someone, someone you love.'

'But that's it, isn't it? Because I was so desperate to love him, and believe he loved me back. I wanted to impress him with how good I could be—as good as he was. I wanted to believe the reason I hardly ever saw him was because he was so busy with his important duties, not because he didn't give a damn. Not because he'd rather screw and spend his way through Europe than spend one unnecessary moment with his son.' He broke off, nearly panting, the old rage and hurt coursing through him so hard and fast he felt as if he couldn't breathe.

And he felt so ashamed—ashamed that it still made him angry, still hurt. Ashamed that Liana knew.

She rose from her desk and he stiffened as she put her arms around him, drew his head to her shoulder as if he was still that desperate, deluded, and disappointed child.

And maybe he was.

'Oh, Sandro.' She was silent for a moment, stroking his hair, and he closed his eyes, revelling in her acceptance, her comfort even as he acknowledged that he didn't deserve it. 'What was the final straw, then?' she asked and he stiffened.

'The final—'

'What was the thing that made you leave?'

He drew a shuddering breath. 'I found out the truth about him when I was eighteen, at university. It was the first time I'd really had any freedom, and everything about it made me start to wonder. Doubt.'

She nodded slowly. 'I know how that feels.'

'And then one afternoon my father's private secretary called me up and asked me to issue a statement that he'd been visiting me that week when he hadn't. It didn't make any sense to me, but I did it. I started really doubting then, though, and the next time I was home I asked my father why he'd wanted me to do that.' He was silent for a moment, recalling the look of impatience on his father's face. 'He'd been with a mistress, some pretty young thing my mother was annoyed about, and he knew there would be a big media fuss if the tabloids got wind of it. He told me all of this so matter-of-factly, without so much as a flicker of guilt or remorse, and I suppose that's when the scales really fell from my eyes.' Sandro let out a long, weary sigh. 'But I didn't actually leave until three years later. Three years of going along with it all, corroborating his stupid stories, lying to the press, to him, to myself, about everything.'

Liana's gaze was wide and dark. 'And then?'

'And then…' He'd told more to this woman than he had to anyone else, and yet he still felt reluctant to reveal all. Reveal himself, and his own weaknesses. 'And then I just couldn't take it anymore. I hated who I'd become. So I told him I was renouncing my inheritance, that I wanted to start my own business and live my own life.' It sounded so selfish, even now, after all these years. 'The funny thing is,' Sandro made himself continue, 'I didn't really mean it.'

He saw surprise flash across Liana's face. 'You didn't?'

'No, I was just—testing him, I suppose. Pushing him. Because I expected him to beg me to stay, admit he loved me and it was all a mistake and— I don't even know.'

He let out a ragged huff of laughter as he raked his hand through his hair. 'How stupid can you be, eh?'

'I don't call that stupid,' Liana said quietly. 'Desperate, maybe.'

'Fine. I was desperate. Desperate and deluded right to the end, because of course he didn't do any of that. He just laughed in my face and told me to go right ahead. He had another son who would do just as well.'

And so he'd gone, proud and defiant and so desperately hurting. He'd gone, and he'd stayed away for fifteen years, only to come back because he'd thought his father had finally seen the light. Would finally admit he was sorry, he'd been wrong, he really did love him.

Blah. Blah. Blah. None of that, of course, had happened. But he'd told Liana enough, and he didn't feel like admitting to that.

'I'm sorry,' Liana whispered, and brushed a kiss across his lips. 'For all of it.'

'So am I.' He kissed her back, needing her touch, her sweetness. Needing to forget all the hurt and anger and disappointment he'd just raked up with his words.

And she did make him forget it; in Liana's arms he didn't feel like the sad, needy boy desperate for love. He didn't feel like a man racked by remorse and guilt for turning his back on his duty. He didn't feel like a king who didn't deserve his crown.

He just felt like a man, a man this amazing, wonderful, vibrant woman loved.

And that was all he wanted to be.

That night Liana lay in bed with Sandro's arm stretched out across her stomach and felt as if the first of the past's ghosts had been banished.

But what about hers?

She recalled Sandro's innocent question, so gently posed. *So Chiara was just one of the unlucky ones?*

She hadn't told Sandro the truth about that. About her. Chiara had been unlucky because she'd had a sister who had gone blank and still and unmoving when she'd needed her most. She'd had Liana.

And while part of her craved to tell Sandro the truth, to have him know and accept her wholeheartedly, the rest of her was too afraid because there were no guarantees. No promises that Sandro would accept her, would love her, if he knew how badly she'd failed someone she'd loved.

Her parents hadn't. Her father hadn't spoken to her for months after Chiara's death; even now he never quite looked at her when they talked. And he never showed her any affection. They'd never been the most demonstrative family—Chiara had cornered the market on that—but since her little sister's death her father hadn't touched her at all. Not one kiss or hug or even brush of the hand.

And could she really blame him?

She was a hypocrite, Liana knew, for wanting Sandro's secrets, his pain and shame and fear, and keeping all of hers back. If she'd been able to accept and love him, why couldn't he do the same for her?

Because your secrets are worse, your sins greater.

And yet not telling him—keeping that essential part of her back—felt like a cancer gnawing at all of her certainties, eating her heart.

How could she keep something so crucial from him?

CHAPTER ELEVEN

SANDRO ATTEMPTED TO listen as one of his cabinet ministers talked, his voice reminding him of the buzzing of a bumblebee that flung itself against the window of one of the palace's meeting rooms. He'd been closeted in here with his cabinet for nearly three hours and he'd barely been able to hear a word that had been said.

All because of Liana.

Ever since he'd unburdened himself to her he'd felt as if they were closer than ever. He loved her more than ever, for simply loving him. And that fact—that they actually loved each other—felt like an incredible blessing, a miracle.

A wonder and a joy.

And yet occasionally, when he glimpsed the shadows in her eyes, the way she'd suddenly turn away, he'd still feel as if she was keeping something from him. Hiding part of herself, but he didn't want to press. Demand answers she might not be ready to give. They had time, after all. Their love was new, perhaps fragile. He wasn't ready to test it in that way.

They had time.

'Your Highness?'

With effort Sandro jerked his gaze back to his expectant cabinet and attempted to focus on the discussion of domestic policy that had been taking up the better part of the afternoon.

'Yes?'

The minister of economic policy cleared his throat. 'We were just going to take a look at the budget Prince Leo proposed....'

Sandro glanced down at the painstakingly and laboriously made list of figures he'd assumed his ministers had put together. Not just Leo.

'Leo drafted this budget?' he asked, heard how sharp his voice sounded. 'When?'

He saw several ministers glance at Leo sitting on the other end of the table and an unease that had been skirting the fringes of his mind for months now suddenly swooped down and grabbed him by the throat. He felt as if he couldn't breathe.

'A few years back, when—' one of the ministers began, glancing uncertainly at Leo, whose face was expressionless, his body still.

'Years,' Sandro repeated, his mind spinning. Years ago, when Leo had thought he would be king.

He turned to stare at his brother, who gazed evenly back. 'I didn't realise you had taken such an interest, Leo,' he murmured. His father would have been alive, of course, and reigning as king. Leo would have been waiting, no more than a reluctant placeholder. Or so Sandro had thought.

But perhaps his brother hadn't been so reluctant, after all.

'I took an interest in all government policy,' Leo answered, and Sandro couldn't tell a thing from his tone. 'Naturally I wanted to be prepared.'

'For when you would become king,' Sandro clarified,

and he felt a silent tension ripple its way around the room, felt it in Leo's body as well as his own.

'Yes.'

The air felt charged, electric. Why hadn't Leo told him this before? Why had he kept it from him, like some damn secret he was the only one who didn't know?

'Perhaps we ought to review your proposals,' Sandro said after a moment. 'I'd be interested in knowing just what they are.'

Something flickered across Leo's face, something sad, almost like grief. 'Of course,' he said. 'I'll have my assistant put all the relevant paperwork in your study.'

They held each other's gaze for a moment longer, a moment that felt taut with tension, almost hostile. Then Sandro broke first, reaching for another sheaf of papers as the meeting went on.

Three hours later Sandro sat in his father's study, dazed by what he had learned and read. What he had never known, even if he should have. Guessed, or at least wondered about.

For fifteen years Leo had thought he would be king. Sandro had been utterly out of the picture, disinherited, as good as forgotten, and Leo would have been preparing for his own kingship, planning on it. And then Sandro had swept in and taken it away without so much as a passing thought for his brother.

He sank onto a chair in his study, his head in his hands. He'd spent the past few hours reading all of Leo's proposals, well-thought-out multi-year plans for industry, economic policy, energy efficiency. After his father's outdated and uninterested reign, Leo had been poised to take Maldinia in a whole new and exciting direction.

Until Sandro had returned and taken it all away from him.

Sandro's mind spun with realisations, with new understanding about the nature of the coolness between him and the brother he'd once loved more than any other person. The brother who had hero-worshipped him as a child. The brother who he had left because he'd been so angry and hurt by his father's contempt and rejection.

The brother, he thought hollowly, who would make an excellent king.

Better than he would.

Why had Leo never told him of his ambitions, his plans? When Sandro had returned, Leo had not made a single protest. He'd stepped aside so quickly Sandro had assumed he'd been relieved to be done of his duty. He'd projected his own feelings onto Leo without ever really considering how his brother might have changed over the past decade and a half.

Yet the uncertainty had always been there, lingering. The fear that Leo would make a better king than he would—deserved to be king more than he did—had always taunted him from the dark corners of his heart and mind.

And now?

Now, Sandro thought numbly, he should step aside and let his brother rule as he'd been intending to for so long. As he deserved to. The cabinet would surely approve; their respect and admiration for Leo and his proposals had been evident in every word they'd spoken this afternoon.

And if Leo were king…Sandro would be free, as he'd claimed he always wanted. He could return to California, take up the reins of his IT firm once more. Be his own man. Live his own life.

Why did the thought make his stomach sour and his fists clench?

He knew why; of course he did. Because of Liana. Liana had married him to become queen. No matter what feelings had since grown between them since then, he could not escape that truth. He couldn't escape the hard reality that their marriage was that of a king and queen, based on convenience and duty. Not a man and woman deeply in love, as much as he might still wish for it. As much as it had felt like that, for the past few weeks.

Weeks. They'd only had weeks together, little more than a handful of days. Put that against fifteen years of Leo working for the monarchy and there was no question. No contest.

A knock sounded on the door and Sandro jerked his head up, blinking the room back into focus. 'Come in.'

'Sandro?' Leo stood in the doorway.

Sandro stared at his brother and felt a pressure build in his chest. Everything inside him felt so tight and aching he could barely force the words out. 'Why didn't you tell me?'

Quietly Leo closed the door, leaned against it. 'Tell you what, exactly?'

'How hard you've been working these past fifteen years—'

Leo raised an eyebrow. 'Did you think I'd been slacking off?'

'No, but—' Sandro raked his hands through his hair, shook his head. 'I thought— I thought— I don't know what I thought.'

'Exactly,' Leo answered, and with a jolt Sandro realised that underneath his brother's unruffled attitude was a deep, latent anger—an anger he was now giving voice to, even as his tone remained steady. 'You didn't think. You haven't thought about me or what I've been doing when you were away for fifteen years, Sandro, and you didn't think about me when you returned.'

Sandro stared at Leo, felt a hot rush of shame sweep over him. 'That's not true, Leo. I did think of you.'

'In passing?' The cynicism in his brother's voice tore at him. 'A moment here or there? You didn't even say goodbye.'

Sandro glanced down. No more excuses. 'I'm sorry,' he said quietly. 'I should have. I should have done it all differently.'

'So why did you leave, out of curiosity?' Leo asked after a moment. 'Did it all just get a bit much for you?'

'I suppose you could say that. I felt— I honestly felt as if I'd lose my soul if I stayed another minute. All the lies, Leo, all the pretending. I couldn't stand it.'

'Neither could I.'

'I know.' Sandro dragged in a breath. 'And I'm sorry if it felt as if I were dumping you in it. But when Father disinherited me— Well, I had no choice then. I had no place here.'

Leo's expression tightened. 'He only disinherited you because you told him you were leaving.'

'I was bluffing,' Sandro confessed flatly. He felt that familiar ache in his chest. 'I was trying to make him admit— Oh, God, I don't even know what. That he needed me. Loved me.' He blinked hard and set his jaw. 'Stupid, I know.'

He couldn't look at Leo, didn't want to see the pity or scorn on his brother's face. 'Not stupid,' Leo said after a moment. 'Naive, maybe, in believing there was anything good in him. He was the most selfish man I ever knew.'

'And I can't believe I didn't see that until I was eighteen years old. You saw through him from the first, didn't you? And I insisted on believing he was a good man. That he loved me.'

Leo shrugged. 'I was always more cynical than you.'

'I am sorry,' Sandro said again, and he felt his regret and remorse with every fibre of his being. He hoped his brother did too. 'I should have reached out to you. Explained. And when I came back I should have asked if you still wanted to be king—'

'It's not a game of pass the parcel, Sandro. Father chose you to be king. He never really wanted me.'

Sandro shook his head. 'That's not true. It was me he didn't want.'

Leo let out a hard bark of laughter. 'Oh? How do you reckon that?'

'He told me. When I threatened to leave. He said he didn't care, I should go right ahead, because he had another son who would do just as well.'

Leo stared at him for a long moment. 'He never acted as if he thought I would,' he finally said. 'He was always telling me how I was second choice, second best, and he only put up with me at all because you were out of the picture.'

Sandro shook his head slowly. 'What a bastard.'

'I know.'

They sat in silence for a moment, but it lacked the tension and hostility of a few moments before. It felt more like grief.

'Even when I came back,' Sandro finally said, the words painful to admit even though he knew Leo needed to hear them, 'he said he'd still rather have you as his heir. It was only because of the media fallout with Alyse that he summoned me.'

'He was just looking for an excuse to get you back.'

'I don't know.' Sandro sat back in his chair, weary and

heartsick at the thought of how their father had manipulated them for so long. Hurt them with his casual cruelty. 'It's all so pointless. Why did he want us both to feel like a second choice? What good would it do?'

'Because he was a weak man and he wanted us to be weak. Strength scared him. If one of us was actually a decent king, his own legacy would look even worse.'

'Maybe so.' They were both silent for a moment, and then, a new heaviness inside him, Sandro spoke again. 'And you would be a good king, Leo, no matter what our father thought.'

Leo just shrugged. 'I would have done my duty, just as you will.'

'I wish I'd known—'

'Do you, really?' There was no anger in Leo's voice, just a certain shrewdness. 'Because you never asked.'

'I know.' His own weakness shamed him. He hadn't asked because he hadn't really wanted to know, no matter what he said now. Hadn't wanted to consider that not only did he not deserve his title, but his brother did. 'I've been ashamed of myself, Leo. For running away all those years ago. For not being strong enough to stay. What kind of king acts like that?'

Leo was silent for a long moment. 'Sometimes it's stronger to go.'

'It didn't feel like strength to me.'

'You did what you needed to do, Sandro. There's no point raking yourself over the coals now. The past is finished.'

'It's not finished,' Sandro said quietly. 'Not yet.'

Leo frowned. 'What do you mean?'

He met his brother's gaze squarely. 'You should be king.'

Leo narrowed his eyes. 'Sandro—'

'I shouldn't have come back,' he continued steadily, as if Leo hadn't even spoken. 'If I hadn't, you'd be king now. All those plans, all those proposals—you'd have put them into place.'

Leo just shrugged again, but Sandro saw a certain tautness to his brother's mouth, a hardness in his eyes. He was right; his brother still wanted to be king. Still *should* be king. 'Tell me, Leo, that there isn't at least a part of you that wants what you deserve. What you'd been preparing for, for half of your life. It's only natural—'

'Fine. Yes.' Leo bit off the words and spat them out. 'I'll admit it. A *part*. It's hard to let go of certain expectations of what you think your life is going to look like. I thought I'd be king, and I wanted to be a damn good one after Father. Then in the matter of a moment it was snatched away from me. I won't pretend that didn't sting a little, Sandro.'

'More than a little.'

'Fine. Yes. What does it matter now?'

'It matters now,' Sandro said quietly, 'because I should abdicate. Let you take the throne as planned.'

Leo's eyebrows shot up. 'Don't be ridiculous—'

'I've only been king for six months. A blip on the radar. The people here don't even know me, except as the brother who ran away.' His smile twisted. 'The prodigal son. I don't know why I didn't see it before. I suppose I was too blinded by my own misery. But it makes sense, Leo. You know it does.'

'I don't know anything of the sort.' Leo's jaw bunched. 'Stop talking nonsense, Sandro.'

'It isn't nonsense—'

'Do you *want* to abdicate?'

He heard curiosity in his brother's voice, but also a certain eagerness, even if Leo would insist otherwise with every breath in his body. Sandro knew better, and he kept his face blank, his voice toneless, as he gave the only answer he could. 'Of course I do. It's the right thing to do. You'd make a better king, and I never wanted to be king anyway. You know that, Leo.' He felt as if the words were tearing great strips off his soul, pieces from his heart, and yet he knew it was the only thing he could say. Could do, even if it meant losing Liana. His brother deserved his rightful place.

And he deserved his.

Woodenly he rose from the desk. 'It shouldn't take long to put it into motion.'

'Sandro, wait. Don't do anything rash—'

'It's not rash. It's obvious to me, Leo. And to you, I think.'

He turned, saw his brother shaking his head, but there was a light in his eyes neither of them could deny. He wanted this. Of course he did.

Smiling, Sandro put a hand on Leo's shoulder. 'I'm happy for you,' he said, and then he left the room.

Liana gazed in the mirror, smoothed a strand of hair away from her forehead and checked that her dress—a full-skirted evening gown in a silvery pink—looked all right.

She heard the door to her bedroom open and saw with a light heart that it was Sandro.

'I was wondering where you were. We're due at the Museum of Fine Art in an hour for the opening of the new wing.' Sandro didn't answer, and she smoothed the skirt of her evening gown. 'I don't know about this dress. Do I look too much like Cinderella?'

'An apt comparison.'

She laughed lightly and shook her head. 'How's that?'

'She found her prince, didn't she? At the ball. And then she lost him again.'

For the first time since he'd entered the room Liana registered his tone: cool and flat. She turned to face him with a frown. 'What's wrong, Sandro?'

He lifted one shoulder in a shrug. 'Nothing's wrong.'

Confusion deepened into unease. Alarm. 'You're acting rather strange.'

'I had an eye-opening cabinet meeting today.'

'Oh?' Liana eyed him warily, noting the almost eerie stillness of his body, the blankness of his face. She hadn't seen him look like this in weeks…since they'd first been strangers to one another, talking marriage. 'Eye-opening?' she repeated cautiously. 'Why don't you tell me about it?'

'The details don't matter,' he dismissed. 'But it's made me realise——' He stopped suddenly, and for a moment the blankness of his face was broken by a look of such anguish that Liana started forward, her hands outstretched.

'Sandro, what is it? What's wrong?'

'I'm planning to abdicate, Liana.'

Sandro watched the shock rush over Liana, making her eyes widen, her face go pale. She looked, he thought heavily, horrified.

'Abdicating?' she finally repeated, her voice little more than a whisper. 'But…why?'

He felt emotions catch in his chest, words lodge in his throat and tangle on his tongue. So far her reaction was far from hopeful. She looked shell-shocked. Devastated. And all because she wouldn't be queen. 'Does it really matter?'

'Of course it matters.'

'Why?' The one word was raw, torn from him. He

stared at her, willing her expression to clear, for her to say it didn't matter, after all. She'd follow him anywhere. She'd love him without a throne or a title or a crown. But why should she say that? She obviously didn't feel it.

She didn't say anything. She just stared at him helplessly, her face pale and shocked as she shook her head slowly. 'Because, Sandro, you're *king*. And I'm your wife.'

'My queen.'

'Yes, your queen! You can't just leave that behind—'

'But I did before, as you've reminded me—'

'I've reminded you? When was the last time I've mentioned that?'

'You haven't forgotten.'

'I don't have amnesia! It's not something you can just forget.'

'Exactly.'

'Why are you thinking of this?' Liana asked, her voice wavering, her expression still dazed. 'It seems so sudden—'

'And unwelcome, obviously.' There could be no mistaking her disappointment, her distress at learning he might no longer be king. And she would no longer be queen.

'Of course it's unwelcome,' Liana said, and Sandro's last frail hope withered to ash. 'We were just starting to build a life here, a life I thought you were happy with—'

'Being king is not my life. It's not *me*.' The words, he knew, had been in his heart, burning in his chest for his whole life. Hadn't he wanted his parents, his friends, *anyone* to see that he was more than this title, this role? Hadn't he wanted just one person in his life to see him as something other than future king, heir apparent?

And obviously Liana didn't. He hated that he'd put

himself out there again. 'But obviously,' he continued, his voice cold and lifeless now, 'you don't feel the same.'

Liana went even paler, even stiller. 'What do you mean?'

'Our marriage doesn't have much point now, does it?' he asked, his mouth forming a horrible parody of a smile. 'If I'm not king, you're not queen.'

Something flashed across her face but he couldn't tell what it was. 'True,' she said, her voice expressionless. She'd assembled her features into a mask, the Madonna face he recognised from when they'd first met, icy and composed. Sandro hated seeing her like that again, when he'd seen her so vibrant and beautiful and alive. So real with him...except perhaps none of it had been real, after all, or at least not real enough.

'And if our marriage has no point,' he forced himself to continue, 'then there's no point to being married.'

He didn't see so much as a flicker on her face. *Damn it,* he thought, *say something. Fight for me. For us.* Here he was, pushing as he always did, practically begging. *Accept me. Love me.* And of course she didn't.

She just remained silent, staring and still. No response at all. Even so Sandro ached to go to her, take her in his arms. Kiss her into responding to him, just as he had when they'd first met. He wanted to demand that she admit the days they had were real, and they could have more. That she could love him even if he weren't king.

Still Liana didn't speak, and with a sound that was somewhere between a sneer and a sob Sandro stalked out of the room.

Liana stood there, unmoving and silent as the door clicked shut. He'd left. In a matter of moments—not much more than a minute—her entire life, all her hope and happiness, had been destroyed.

Just as before.

Just as when Chiara had choked to death and she'd watched and done nothing. Been unable to do anything, and that appalling lack of action would haunt her for all of her days.

And had she learned nothing in the past twenty years? Once again she'd let her own stunned silence damn her. She had seen from Sandro's expression that he wanted something from her—but what? As she'd stared at him, his expression so horribly blank, she'd had no idea what it was. And while her mind spun and her body remained still, he walked out of her room.

Out of her life.

As if the realisation had kick-started her, she suddenly jerked to life, strode to the door, and wrenched it open. Sandro was halfway down the hallway, his bearing straight and proud as he walked away from her.

'Stop right there, Sandro.'

He stiffened, stilled, then slowly turned around. 'I don't think we have anything more to say to each other.'

'You don't *think*?' Liana repeated in disbelief. She grabbed handfuls of her frothy dress as she strode towards him, full of sudden, consuming rage. 'You just drop that bombshell on me and walk out of my life with hardly a word, and you think that's *it*?' Her voice shook and tears started in her eyes, although she didn't know whether they were of anger or grief. 'You told me you *loved* me, Sandro. Was that a lie?'

'You told me the same,' he answered coolly.

She stared at him for a moment, trying to fathom what had brought him to this decision. 'I think I get it,' she finally said slowly. 'This is another ultimatum.'

'Another—'

'Just like with your father.'

'Don't—'

'Don't what? Don't tell the truth? You threatened to leave once before, Sandro, with your father all those years ago. You wanted him to admit he loved you and he didn't. He disappointed you and so you left, and now you're doing the same to me, threatening me—'

'It wasn't a *threat.*'

'Maybe you don't think it was. Maybe you are seriously considering abdicating. But you didn't come to me as a husband, Sandro. As a—a lover and a friend. You didn't sit me down and tell me what was on your mind, in your heart, and what I might think about it. No, you just walk in and drop your damned bomb and then leave before the debris has even cleared.'

'Your response was obvious—'

'Oh, really? Because as I recall I didn't say much of anything. I was still processing it all and you decided that meant I couldn't love you if you weren't king. You jumped to so many damn conclusions you made my head spin.' And her heart break.

Sandro folded his arms. 'You made your reasons for our marriage clear, Liana. You wanted to be queen—'

'You're going to throw that at me? After everything we've said and done and felt?' She shook her head, her throat too thick with tears to speak. Finally she got some words out. 'Damn you, Sandro. Damn you for only thinking about your feelings and not mine.'

A muscle flickered in his jaw. 'So you're denying it?'

'Denying what?'

'That you married me to become queen—'

'No, of course not. That is why I chose to marry you. There were a lot of messed-up reasons behind that choice,

but what I am trying to say—what I thought you knew—
is that I've *changed*. As I thought you had changed, except maybe you didn't because I thought you were a
cold-hearted bastard when I met you, and you certainly
seem like one now.' He blinked, said nothing, and the
floodgates of Liana's soul burst open. She drew in a wet,
revealing breath.

'I never told you about Chiara's death.'

He blinked again, clearly surprised, maybe discomfited. 'You told me she choked—'

'Yes, she had a seizure and she choked on her own
vomit. But what I didn't tell you was that I was there.
The only one there. My parents were away and our nanny
was busy. I was alone in the room with her and I watched
her choke and I couldn't move to help her. Couldn't even
speak. I panicked, Sandro, so badly that it caused my
sister's death. I could have run to her, could have called
for help, and instead I was frozen to the floor with shock
and fear.' She felt her chest go tight and her vision tun-
nel as in her mind's eye Chiara's desperate face stared
up at her in mute appeal. And she'd simply stood there,
wringing her hands. 'By the time I finally got myself to
move, it was too late.' She'd run to her, turned her over.
Cleared out her mouth with her own scrabbling fingers,
sobbing her sister's name. And Chiara had just stared
lifelessly back. *Too late.*

Liana drew in another ragged breath. 'I as good as
killed her, Sandro, and I'll live with that for my whole
life.' She realised, distantly, that tears were running down
her face but she didn't care. Didn't wipe them away. 'And
when you delivered your awful ultimatum, I froze again.
Didn't speak. Didn't move. But damn if I'm going to lose
my soul again, Sandro, because I didn't have the courage
or the presence of mind to do something.'

She stepped closer to him, close enough to poke him in the chest. 'I love you. You love me. At least I hope you do, after what I just told you—'

He shook his head, his own eyes bright. 'Do you really think something like that would make me change my mind?'

'I don't know. It changed my parents' minds. At least, it felt like that. We've never recovered. I never recovered, because I spent the past twenty years living my life as an apology and cloaking myself in numbness because feeling meant feeling all the guilt and shame and fear, and I couldn't do that and survive.'

'Liana—' Sandro's face was twisted with anguish, but she wasn't done.

'So we love each other, then, and I might not know much about love but I do know that when you love someone, you believe the best of them. You don't wait for them to let you down. You don't set up situations so they fail. Maybe you've been looking for love for most of your life, Sandro, since you didn't get it from your parents. Guess what? I didn't get it either. My father has barely looked at me since Chiara died. But even I know enough to realise that you don't find love when you act like it's going to disappoint you. When you don't trust it or the person who is meant to love you for five minutes of honest conversation.' She shook her head, empty now, so terribly empty. 'You think I disappointed you by not saying something when you wanted me to. Well, you know what, Sandro? *You* disappointed *me*.'

And with another hopeless shake of her head, she turned and walked back down the hall, away from him.

CHAPTER TWELVE

HE'D SCREWED UP. Big time. It was nearing midnight and Sandro sat in his study, gazing broodingly into space.

Every word Liana had spoken was true.

He had given her an ultimatum, been testing her and the truth of her feelings. It had been an arrogant and appalling thing to do, and, worst of all, he'd been so self-righteous about it.

And while he hadn't had the courage to be honest with her, she'd possessed more than enough to be honest with him. He thought of what she'd admitted about her sister and felt tears sting his eyes.

He was such a bastard.

It had taken him all of ten seconds to realise just how wrong he was, but ten seconds was too long because Liana had already locked her bedroom door, and she wouldn't answer it when he hammered on it and asked her—begged her—to let him in.

He'd hated feeling as if he was begging for love or just simple affection from his parents, hated how as a child he'd always tried to get his father to notice him. But he didn't care now how desperate or foolish or pathetic he looked. He'd go down on his knees to beg his wife to forgive him. He just wanted to be given the chance.

He heard the door to his study open and lurched forwards, hoping against all the odds that it was Liana.

It wasn't. It was Leo.

'Sandro,' he said, unsmiling. 'What the hell did you do?'

'What do you mean?'

'Half the palace could hear Liana shouting at you. And she doesn't shout.'

'I told her I was abdicating.'

Leo stared at him for a long moment. 'Sandro,' he finally said, 'you are a damned idiot.'

Sandro tried to smile, but it felt as if his face were cracking apart. 'I know.'

Leo stepped forward. 'And so am I.'

'What do you mean?'

'I don't want you to abdicate, Sandro. I don't want to be king.'

Sandro shook his head. 'I saw it in your eyes—'

Leo shook his head impatiently. 'Oh, screw that. Yes, as I told you before, there is a part of me that feels hard done by. Disappointed. I'll get over it, Sandro. I'm a big boy. So are you. And you have spent the past six months working yourself to the bloody bone to prove what a good king you are. A great king. You're the only one who doesn't think so.'

'No, I don't,' Sandro said in a low voice. He closed his eyes briefly. It was the first time he'd admitted it out loud.

'And why is that? Why don't you think you'll make— *you are*—a good king?'

Sandro didn't answer for a long moment. Admitting so much to anyone, especially Leo, who had once idolised him, was painful. 'Because,' he finally said in a low voice, 'I shirked my duty, didn't I? I ran away.'

'And you came back.'

'After fifteen years—'

'So? Is there a time limit? And running away—if you really want to call it that—seemed like your only choice back then.' Leo's voice roughened with emotion. 'I believe that, Sandro, even if I've acted like I didn't because I was hurt. I know you wouldn't have left me like that unless you felt you had to.'

Sandro felt his eyes fill. 'I wouldn't have,' he said, his voice choked as he blinked hard. 'I swear to you, Leo, I wouldn't have.'

They stared at each other, faces full of emotion, the air thick with both regret and forgiveness.

Finally Leo smiled, and Sandro did too. 'Well, then,' he said. 'You see?'

Sandro dragged a hand over his eyes. 'I'm not sure I see anything.'

'Leave behind the bitterness and anger, Sandro. Forget about how Mother and Father raised us, how they treated the monarchy. Usher in a new kingdom, begin a new era. You can do it.'

'And what about you?'

'Like I said, I'll get over it. And to be honest, I'm a little relieved. I admit, when you first came back, I was shocked. Hurt too, if I'm honest, because after fifteen years of working myself to the bone to prove myself to our father, he cast me aside at the first opportunity. But I've already promised myself not to live steeped in bitterness or regret, Sandro, and in their own way things have worked out for the best. I'm happy not to be in the spotlight. So is Alyse. We've spent a hell of a long time there, and it wasn't very pleasant.'

'And what of your ambitions? Your plans?'

With a wry smile Leo gestured to the papers scattered

across the desk. 'Feel free to use them. And consult me anytime. My fees are quite reasonable.'

Sandro felt something unfurl inside him, a kind of fragile, incredulous hope. 'I don't know,' he said and Leo just smiled.

'No one does, do they? No one knows what's going to work, what's going to happen. But you have my support, and Alyse's, and the cabinet's.' He paused. 'And you have Liana's, but you might have to grovel a bit to get it back.'

To his amazement Sandro felt a small smile quirk his mouth. 'There's no might about it,' he answered. 'That's a definite.'

'So what are you waiting for?'

'She won't see me.'

'She's angry and hurt. Give her a little time.'

Sandro nodded, even though he didn't want to give her time. Didn't want to wait. He wanted to break her door down and demand that she listen to him. Tell her what an ass he'd been and how much he loved her.

He just needed to find a way to make her listen.

Liana stood in her bedroom with its spindly chairs and feminine décor and stared out of the window at the gardens now in full, glorious spring. The roses were just beginning to unfurl, their petals silky and fragrant. Everything was coming to life, and she felt as if she was dead inside.

She had barely slept last night, had tossed and turned and tormented herself with all the what-ifs. What if she'd said something when Sandro had wanted her to? What if she'd let him back in when he'd knocked on her door and asked her to talk to him?

But she couldn't talk; she felt too empty and grief-stricken for words. She'd given Sandro everything. *Ev-*

erything. And he hadn't loved her enough to wait five minutes—five *seconds*—to explain. Say something. Do something.

And what had he done but judge her and jump to conclusions? Was that what love was?

If so, she was better off without it. Without him.

Even if her heart felt like some raw, wounded thing, pulsing painfully inside her. It would heal. She would. She didn't want to go back to numbness, but maybe she'd go back a *little*. Feel a little less. Eventually.

And as for her marriage? Sandro was right; if he wasn't king, she didn't need to be queen. They certainly didn't need to stay married for convenience's sake. He didn't need an heir, after all, and maybe he wanted to return to his life in California. Maybe he didn't want her anymore. Maybe her confession about Chiara had made him despise her.

Yet the thought of actually divorcing was too awful to contemplate. Maybe they would simply live as strangers, seeing as little of each other as possible, just as she'd envisioned a lifetime ago. Just as she'd *wanted*.

The thought was almost laughable, ridiculous; she certainly didn't want it now. But after the debacle of their confrontation last night, she wasn't sure how they could go on.

Behind her she heard the door open and she drew a shuddering breath. She'd asked Rosa to bring her breakfast to her room because she couldn't face seeing everyone—much less Sandro—in the dining room.

'Liana.'

Everything in her tensed at the sound of Sandro's voice. She turned, saw he was carrying her breakfast tray. She shook her head.

'Don't, Sandro.' Although she wasn't sure what she

was asking him not to do. *Don't break my heart, fragile thing that it is, again.*

'Don't what?' he asked quietly. 'Don't say I'm sorry?'

She drew a shuddering breath. 'Are you?'

'Unbelievably so. More than I've ever been, for anything, in my life.'

She shook her head. It wasn't that simple, that easy. 'Why did you do that to me?'

'Because I'm a stupid, selfish idiot.'

'I'm serious, Sandro.'

'So am I.' With a sad smile he put the breakfast tray down on the table by her bed. He gestured at one of the silver dishes on the tray. 'Strawberries. No chocolate, though.'

Liana just folded her arms. 'I want answers, Sandro.'

'And I'll tell you. You know how you thought you looked like Cinderella last night?'

She eyed him warily; she had no idea where he was going with this. 'Yes....'

'You are Cinderella, Liana. You came to the castle to marry a prince, except in this case the said prince was a king and he wasn't all that charming. He was kind of an ass, actually.'

A smile twitched at her mouth even though she still felt heavy inside. 'Was he? Why?'

'Because he was so consumed with how frustrated he felt and all the things he wanted out of life that he didn't have and how no one loved him. Pathetic, whingy little so-and-so, really.'

'I think you might be being a little hard on him.'

'No, he definitely was. He never thought about what other people might be feeling, especially his Cinderella.'

Her mouth curved again in a tremulous smile, almost

of its own volition. 'I wouldn't say he was *quite* that self-absorbed.'

'He was worse,' Sandro answered. 'Cinderella couldn't find that pointy glass slipper because it was stuck up his ass.'

She let out a sudden, startled laugh. *'Sandro—'*

'He had no idea what he was doing or how much he was hurting people.' He took a step towards her, a sad, whimsical smile on his face. 'Seriously, Liana, he was a mess.'

'And what happened?'

'Cinderella woke him up with a good old slap. Yanked her shoe out and made him realise just how self-important and stupid he was being—about a lot of things. Her. His family. His past. Himself.'

'And?' she asked softly.

'And he only hopes he can still make it right.' He took another step towards her, and he was close enough to touch. She almost did. 'I hope I can make it right, Liana, by telling you how wrong I've been. How unbelievably, unbearably stupid and selfish.' The smile he gave her was shaky, vulnerable, and it made her yearn. She shook her head, not ready to surrender even though another part of her ached to.

'You hurt me, Sandro.'

'I know. I was so afraid of being pushed away again. Rejected. And instead I did exactly what you said. I set up a situation where I'd force you to fail, because it was better than feeling like a failure myself. I'm so sorry.'

Liana felt the burn of tears beneath her lids. 'I forgive you.'

'Enough to take me back?'

She wanted him back. Wanted his arms around her,

her head on his shoulder, the steady thud of his heart against her cheek. 'You can't ever do that again.'

'I won't.'

'I know we'll argue, Sandro, I'm not saying we can't disagree or get angry or annoyed or what have you. But you can't—you can't set me up like that. Make me feel like a failure.' Her throat clogged and she blinked hard. 'Because I've felt like that before, and I don't ever want to feel it again.'

'Oh, Liana. Sweetheart.' He took her in his arms then, and she went, pressing her cheek against his shoulder just as she'd longed to. 'I'm sorry for what you endured with your sister,' he whispered, and the first tears started to spill.

'It was my fault.'

'No, it wasn't.'

'Didn't you listen—?'

'I listened, Liana. And I heard a woman who has been torturing herself for two decades about something that was an accident. You were eight years old, Liana, and you were in shock. Where was that nanny anyway?'

'I don't know.'

'If anyone should feel guilty—'

'But I should have done something. I could have—'

'Did you love your sister?'

'More than anything—'

'Then how can you blame yourself for something that was out of your control? If you could have saved her, you would have. The fact that you didn't meant you weren't able to. You didn't know how. You panicked, you froze, yes, but you were *eight*, Liana, a child. And someone else should have been there.'

She shook her head, her tears falling freely now. 'It's not that easy.'

'No, it isn't. But if you can forgive me, then you can forgive yourself. For your own sake, Liana, as well as mine. Because I love you so very much and I can't stand the thought of this guilt eating away at you until there's nothing left.' He eased back from her, gazed down at her with eyes that shone silver. 'I love you. I love your strength and your grace and even your composure that terrified and annoyed me in turns when we first met. I love how you've stepped so beautifully into being a queen my country—our country—is starting to love, just as I love you.'

His words dazed her so much she could hardly speak. Finally she fastened on to the one thing that seemed least important, least overwhelming. 'But I'm not queen anymore.'

'Yes, you are.' The smile he gave her now was crooked and he reached out to brush at her damp cheeks. 'I'm not going to abdicate. I spoke to Leo, and he talked some sense into me. I realised I was thinking of it because I've felt so much guilt and regret about leaving. Running away. And then I was about to do it again.' He shook his head, his thumbs tracing the lines of her cheekbones, wiping away her tears. 'Do you think you're willing to stay married to such a slow learner? A slow learner who loves you quite desperately?'

'Of course I am.' Liana's lips trembled as she tried to smile. 'I'm a bit of a slow learner, myself. I love you, Sandro, but it scared me for a long time, to feel that much, never mind admitting it. But I do love you. So very much.'

He framed her face with his hands, brought her closer to him so her forehead rested against his. They stayed that way for a moment, neither of them speaking, everything in Liana aching with emotion and a new, deeper happiness than she'd ever felt before. A happiness based on total honesty, deep and abiding love.

'We're quite a pair, aren't we?' he murmured. 'Wanting love and being afraid of it at the same time.'

She pressed one hand to his cheek, revelling in the feel of him, and the fact that he was here, that he'd come back and he loved her. 'Love *is* pretty scary,' she said, a smile in her voice, and Sandro nodded, his forehead bumping against hers.

'Terrifying, frankly.'

She let out a shaky laugh and put her arms around him. 'Definitely terrifying. But I do love you, Sandro.'

'And I love you.' He kissed her gently on the lips, a promise and a seal. 'And since it seems that we're both slow learners, it will take us a long time to figure this love out. I think,' he continued as he drew her closer and deepened the kiss, 'it will take the rest of our lives.'

EPILOGUE

One year later

LIANA SMOOTHED THE satin skirt of the gown, admired the admittedly over-the-top ruffles of lace that fell to the floor.

She turned to Sandro with a smile and a shake of her head. 'I can't believe you wore this.'

'If I'd been a little more self-aware at the time, I'm sure I would have been mortified.'

'Well, you were only three months old,' she teased. 'Isabella seems to like it, at any rate.'

'She's a smart girl.'

They both gazed down at their daughter, Isabella Chiara Alexa Diomedi, her eyes already turning the silvergrey of her father's, her dimpled smile reminding Liana with a bittersweet joy of her sister.

With a smile for her daughter, Liana scooped her up and held her against her shoulder, breathed in her warm baby scent.

'Careful,' Sandro warned. 'You just fed her and she likes to give a little bit of that back.' He gave a mock grimace. 'I should know. The palace dry-cleaning bill has skyrocketed since this little one's arrival.'

'I don't mind.'

There was nothing she minded about taking care of her daughter. She was just so happy, so incredulously grateful, to have the opportunity. Isabella's birth had been, in its own way, a healing; no one could replace Chiara, but her daughter's birth had eased the long-held grief of losing her sister.

A gentle knock sounded on the door, and then her mother poked her head in. 'May I come in?'

Liana felt herself tense. Her parents had arrived last night for Isabella's christening; she hadn't actually seen them save for a few formal functions since her wedding. And as usual when she saw her mother, she felt the familiar rush of guilt and regret, tempered now by Sandro's love and her daughter's presence, but still there. Already she could hear the note of apology creep into her voice.

'Of course, Mother. We're just getting Isabella ready for the ceremony.'

Gabriella Aterno stepped into the room, her features looking fragile and faded as always, her smile hesitant and somehow sad.

Sandro stepped forward. 'Would you like to hold her?'

'Oh—may I?'

'Of course,' Liana said, and, with her heart full of too many emotions to name, she handed her daughter to her mother.

Gabriella looked down into Isabella's tiny, impish face and let out a ragged little laugh. 'She has Chiara's dimples.'

Liana felt a flash of shock; her mother had not mentioned Chiara once since her sister's funeral. Twenty-one years of silence.

'She does,' she agreed quietly. 'And her smile.'

'Perhaps she'll have her dark curls.' Gently Gabriella fingered Isabella's wispy, dark hair. 'You two were always so different in looks. No one would have thought you were sisters, save for the way you loved each other.' She looked up then, her eyes shining with tears, the grief naked in her face, and Liana knew how much just those few sentences had cost her.

'Oh, Mother,' she whispered. She swallowed past the tightness in her throat. 'I'm so sorry—'

'I'm sorry Chiara isn't here to see her niece,' Gabriella said. 'But I like to think she still sees, from somewhere.'

'Me too.' Liana blinked hard, focused on her daughter in her mother's arms, and said what had been burning inside her for too many years. 'I'm sorry I didn't save her.'

Gabriella jerked her head up, her eyes wide with shock. 'Save her? Liana, you were eight years old.'

'I know, but I was there.' Liana blinked hard, but it was too late. The tears came anyway. 'I saw— I *watched*—'

'And you've blamed yourself all this time,' Gabriella said softly. 'Oh, my dear.'

'Of course I blamed myself,' Liana answered, batting uselessly at the tears that trickled down her cheeks. 'And you blamed me too, Mother, and Father as well. I'm not angry—I understand why—' She choked on the words, felt Sandro's comforting hand on her shoulder, and she pressed her cheek against it, closed her eyes against the rush of pain and tried to will the tears back.

'Liana, my dear, we blamed ourselves,' Gabriella confessed, her voice trembling with emotion. 'Of course we did—we were her parents. She was our responsibility, not yours.'

Liana opened her eyes, stared at her mother's grief-stricken face. 'But you never said anything,' she whispered. 'Father hasn't even so much as hugged me since—'

'We didn't like to talk about it,' Gabriella told her. 'As

I'm sure you realised. Not because of you, though, but because of us. We felt so wretchedly guilty. I still do.'

'Oh, Mother, no—' Impulsively and yet instinctively Liana went to put her arms around Gabriella, the baby between them.

'All three of us have been consumed by guilt, it seems,' Gabriella said with a sniff. 'And I know your father and I didn't handle it properly back then, or ever. We should have been there for you, spoken to you about it, helped you to grieve. We were too wrapped up in our own pain, and I'm sorry for that.' She shook her head slowly, her eyes still bright with tears. 'I'm sorry I didn't realise how much you blamed yourself. I just assumed—' Her mother drew in a quick breath. 'Assumed you blamed me.'

Liana shook her head. 'No, never.'

They were both silent for a moment, struggling with these new revelations and the emotions they called up. In Gabriella's arms Isabella stirred, gurgled, and then gave her grandmother a big, drooly smile.

Gabriella let out a choked cry of surprise and joy. She turned to Liana with a tear trickling down one pale cheek. 'Then maybe this is a new start for all of us, Liana,' she said, her voice wavering, and Liana nodded and smiled.

She knew there was more to be said, to be confessed and explained and forgiven, but for now she revelled in the second chance they'd all been granted. A second chance at happiness, at love, at life itself.

Gabriella handed the baby back to Sandro and slipped down to the chapel where the christening would be held. Liana gazed at her husband and daughter and felt her heart might burst with so much feeling. She felt so much now, all the emotions she'd denied herself for so long. Joy and wonder, grief and sorrow. She wouldn't keep herself from feeling any of it ever again.

'I couldn't have imagined any of this before I met you,' she said softly. 'Talking to my mother so honestly. Having a husband and child of my own. Loving someone as much as I love you. You've changed me, Sandro.'

'And you've changed me. Thank God.' He smiled wryly and then, with the expertise of a father of a baby, he shifted Isabella to his other shoulder and drew Liana towards him for a kiss. 'This really is the beginning, Liana,' he said softly as he kissed her again. 'Of everything.'

* * * * *

ROMANCE

A Prize Beyond Jewels	Carole Mortimer
A Queen for the Taking?	Kate Hewitt
Pretender to the Throne	Maisey Yates
An Exception to His Rule	Lindsay Armstrong
The Sheikh's Last Seduction	Jennie Lucas
Enthralled by Moretti	Cathy Williams
The Woman Sent to Tame Him	Victoria Parker
What a Sicilian Husband Wants	Michelle Smart
Waking Up Pregnant	Mira Lyn Kelly
Holiday with a Stranger	Christy McKellen
The Returning Hero	Soraya Lane
Road Trip With the Eligible Bachelor	Michelle Douglas
Safe in the Tycoon's Arms	Jennifer Faye
Awakened By His Touch	Nikki Logan
The Plus-One Agreement	Charlotte Phillips
For His Eyes Only	Liz Fielding
Uncovering Her Secrets	Amalie Berlin
Unlocking the Doctor's Heart	Susanne Hampton

MEDICAL

Waves of Temptation	Marion Lennox
Risk of a Lifetime	Caroline Anderson
To Play with Fire	Tina Beckett
The Dangers of Dating Dr Carvalho	Tina Beckett

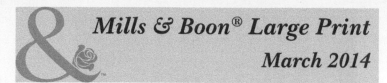

Mills & Boon® Large Print
March 2014

ROMANCE

Million Dollar Christmas Proposal	Lucy Monroe
A Dangerous Solace	Lucy Ellis
The Consequences of That Night	Jennie Lucas
Secrets of a Powerful Man	Chantelle Shaw
Never Gamble with a Caffarelli	Melanie Milburne
Visconti's Forgotten Heir	Elizabeth Power
A Touch of Temptation	Tara Pammi
A Little Bit of Holiday Magic	Melissa McClone
A Cadence Creek Christmas	Donna Alward
His Until Midnight	Nikki Logan
The One She Was Warned About	Shoma Narayanan

HISTORICAL

Rumours that Ruined a Lady	Marguerite Kaye
The Major's Guarded Heart	Isabelle Goddard
Highland Heiress	Margaret Moore
Paying the Viking's Price	Michelle Styles
The Highlander's Dangerous Temptation	Terri Brisbin

MEDICAL

The Wife He Never Forgot	Anne Fraser
The Lone Wolf's Craving	Tina Beckett
Sheltered by Her Top-Notch Boss	Joanna Neil
Re-awakening His Shy Nurse	Annie Claydon
A Child to Heal Their Hearts	Dianne Drake
Safe in His Hands	Amy Ruttan

0214 GEN STD LP

Mills & Boon® Hardback

April 2014

ROMANCE

A D'Angelo Like No Other	Carole Mortimer
Seduced by the Sultan	Sharon Kendrick
When Christakos Meets His Match	Abby Green
The Purest of Diamonds?	Susan Stephens
Secrets of a Bollywood Marriage	Susanna Carr
What the Greek's Money Can't Buy	Maya Blake
The Last Prince of Dahaar	Tara Pammi
The Sicilian's Unexpected Duty	Michelle Smart
One Night with Her Ex	Lucy King
The Secret Ingredient	Nina Harrington
Her Soldier Protector	Soraya Lane
Stolen Kiss From a Prince	Teresa Carpenter
Behind the Film Star's Smile	Kate Hardy
The Return of Mrs Jones	Jessica Gilmore
Her Client from Hell	Louisa George
Flirting with the Forbidden	Joss Wood
The Last Temptation of Dr Dalton	Robin Gianna
Resisting Her Rebel Hero	Lucy Ryder

MEDICAL

200 Harley Street: Surgeon in a Tux	Carol Marinelli
200 Harley Street: Girl from the Red Carpet	Scarlet Wilson
Flirting with the Socialite Doc	Melanie Milburne
His Diamond Like No Other	Lucy Clark

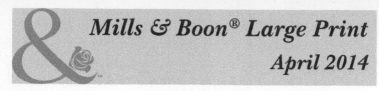

Mills & Boon® Large Print
April 2014

ROMANCE

Defiant in the Desert	Sharon Kendrick
Not Just the Boss's Plaything	Caitlin Crews
Rumours on the Red Carpet	Carole Mortimer
The Change in Di Navarra's Plan	Lynn Raye Harris
The Prince She Never Knew	Kate Hewitt
His Ultimate Prize	Maya Blake
More than a Convenient Marriage?	Dani Collins
Second Chance with Her Soldier	Barbara Hannay
Snowed in with the Billionaire	Caroline Anderson
Christmas at the Castle	Marion Lennox
Beware of the Boss	Leah Ashton

HISTORICAL

Not Just a Wallflower	Carole Mortimer
Courted by the Captain	Anne Herries
Running from Scandal	Amanda McCabe
The Knight's Fugitive Lady	Meriel Fuller
Falling for the Highland Rogue	Ann Lethbridge

MEDICAL

Gold Coast Angels: A Doctor's Redemption	Marion Lennox
Gold Coast Angels: Two Tiny Heartbeats	Fiona McArthur
Christmas Magic in Heatherdale	Abigail Gordon
The Motherhood Mix-Up	Jennifer Taylor
The Secret Between Them	Lucy Clark
Craving Her Rough Diamond Doc	Amalie Berlin

Discover more romance at

www.millsandboon.co.uk

- ❤ WIN great prizes in our exclusive competitions
- ❤ BUY new titles before they hit the shops
- ❤ BROWSE new books and REVIEW your favourites
- ❤ SAVE on new books with the Mills & Boon® Bookclub™
- ❤ DISCOVER new authors

PLUS, to chat about your favourite reads, get the latest news and find special offers:

- 📘 Find us on facebook.com/millsandboon
- 🐦 Follow us on twitter.com/millsandboonuk
- ❤ Sign up to our newsletter at millsandboon.co.uk